PENGUIN BOOKS

TSOTSI

Athol Fugard, South Africa's foremost playwright, was born in Middelburg, Cape Province, in 1932. As a man of the theatre he has written, and directed and acted in — both in South Africa and abroad — over a dozen of his own scripts. Although resident and working in Port Elizabeth (the scene of plays like *Hello and Goodbye* and *Boesman and Lena*) his works are performed widely in the English-speaking world, and in translation. His other plays include *The Blood Knot*, *Sizwe Bansi is Dead*, *The Island*, *Statements after an Arrest under the Immorality Act* and *A Lesson from Aloes*. *Tsotsi* is his first — and thus far — only novel.

ATHOL FUGARD

TSOTSI

PENGUIN BOOKS

Penguin Books Ltd, Harmondsworth, Middlesex, England
Viking Penguin Inc., 40 West 23rd Street, New York, New York 10010, U.S.A.
Penguin Books Australia Ltd, Ringwood, Victoria, Australia
Penguin Books Canada Limited, 2801 John Street, Markham, Ontario, Canada L3R 1B4
Penguin Books (N.Z.) Ltd, 182–190 Wairau Road, Auckland 10, New Zealand

First published in South Africa by Ad. Donker (Pty) Ltd 1980
First published in the United States of America by
Random House, Inc., 1980
Published in Penguin Books 1983, 1986

Printed and bound in Great Britain by
Cox & Wyman Ltd, Reading
Filmset in Photina by
Northumberland Press Ltd, Gateshead

— 1 —

There had been a silence, as always happened at about the same time, a long silence when none of them moved except maybe to lift up a glass and hold it high over their heads for the dregs to drip into their open mouths, or to yawn and stretch and then slump back into their chairs, when one of them might scratch himself, another consider the voice of the woman in the backyard, the old woman who was scolding, rattling her words like stones in a tin, and all of them in their own time looking at the street outside, and the shadows, wondering if they were not yet long enough. It was not a deliberate silence; there was no reason for it, being at first just the pause between something said and the next remark, but growing from that because they were suddenly all without any more words. It ended, as always happened at about the same time, when the young one, the youngest of the four, the one who had said the least, who had sat there and listened to the other three, the one they called Tsotsi, leant forward and brought his slim, delicate hands together, the fingers interlocking in the manner of prayer. The other three looked up at him and waited.

Before that the one called Boston had been telling his story. Boston always had a story. He started early in the afternoon when they came together in Tsotsi's room and settled down with the first bottle of beer, telling it from then for a long time, almost to the hour when the shadows were long enough and Tsotsi told them what they would be doing that night. He told it slowly, taking his time, the words coming in a easy rhythm between the swallows of beer, the belches, the bother of opening another bottle and the other interruptions like leaving the room for the backyard where you rested against the hot corrugated iron fence with an outstretched arm and pissed into the sand, and watched it soak up and dry away before you had left the spot. When he got back he would ask, where was I, and sometimes someone remembered and most times no one cared because it wasn't important. All that mattered was that his voice filled that last reluctant hour of an afternoon that was heavy with the weight of idle hands. They toyed with their glasses, they drew out the wet rings left by the beer bottles into strange patterns on the table-top, while Boston with a gesture that was becoming habitual rubbed his eyes with the thumb and forefinger of his right hand. It was a strain to be without glasses.

The other two were mostly listeners. Die Aap, so called because of his long arms – his knuckles seemed to drag in the dust – listened attentively to every word. Sometimes he had something to say, or asked a question, and he laboured a lot in finding words and putting them together. The last of the four, the one called Butcher, built like Tsotsi with lithe supple bones, but different in his small, dangerous eyes and his pendulous lower lip, Butcher also listened, but with impatience. Why all the words? His stories were told in ten words or less. But there was nothing else to do except listen.

Boston's stories were of no consequence. The time he did this, where he did it and how and with whom ...

A hawker with a pushcart trundles past in the street outside. They see the shadow long after the man has disappeared.

Or the time this happened and why it did and how that happening started off a lot of other things that unfold one after the interminable other in the effortless drone of Boston's voice.

A window of the house across the street, which they can see clearly through their open door, the window burns fiercely with the reflected light of the sun. It must be low. Not long now.

Or that man. That strange man of a time back who went there and never returned.

The old woman is shaking her tin of scolding words in the backyard. A child cries.

Butcher shifts with a sudden spasm of impatience.

Why? Why? Die Aap is asking a question. Boston laughs. 'Because ...' Another bottle comes up from under the table. They fill their glasses. 'Because,' Boston continues, 'because of this cherry. Ja man. Buggered him up she did.'

This then being the pause, and then more than the pause because it was also the end of the story and no one had any more words, and they sat silent a long time until the youngest of the four, the one they called Tsotsi, until suddenly his hands were together and the other three looking at him and waiting.

Boston smiled, Butcher twisted in another spasm of impatience and hate for the silent man, Die Aap waited impassively.

Tsotsi saw it all. The smile that hid fear, the eyes that hid hate, the face that hid nothing. You I can trust, he said to himself, looking at Die Aap. You I must never turn my back on, and it was Butcher he looked at. And you, Boston. You smile at me and your smile hides fear.

'What's it Tsotsi?' Boston asked. He held Tsotsi's gaze for a few seconds, but when the muscles at the end of his mouth began to stiffen he looked down into his empty glass.

'Ja. What's it man?' Butcher asked.

Die Aap remained silent.

'It's Friday night,' Tsotsi said, and looked out of the door. The shadows were long enough. It would soon be dark.

'The trains,' he said. 'Let's take one on the trains.'

Butcher was the first to react. He smiled and then laughed, a cold sound, sharp as a knife blade. 'Ja man. One on the trains,' he said.

But it was Boston that Tsotsi was watching, and Boston knew it and he kept his eyes down, no longer seeing the glass in his hands. But even like that Tsotsi could see his forehead and that was enough because very soon the first film of sweat was shining there.

Die Aap needed time. He repeated what Tsotsi had said. 'The trains. Let's take one on the trains.' He thought about it, framed the picture, his part in it. It was simple. He knew it all. He nodded. 'Ja.' That was all he had to say.

Boston looked up. All three were watching him now.

'Why?' he asked, and played nervously with the glass between his hands.

'Why not?' Tsotsi's voice had an edge.

Boston shrugged his shoulders, tried to yawn but it didn't work. So he sighed, as if bored. 'Sometimes you pick one and he's got nothing.'

Tsotsi let him wait for the reply. 'I never make a mistake.'

Die Aap nodded. 'That's true. Not once.'

Butcher moved with impatience in his seat. Why all the talk. He liked it. 'It's good man. Ja man. It's good.' He stood up. 'Let's go.'

But Tsotsi was still waiting for Boston, still watching him and his elusive eyes, his dry lips, his pink tongue as he tried to moisten them. Boston found nothing else to say against the idea, nothing that they would understand and maybe accept. 'Okay,' he said, 'okay,' so they all stood up and waited while Tsotsi put on his coat, and then followed him out of the room and into the street, Die Aap second then Boston who was saying, 'Okay,' saying it many times between sighs and forced yawns and exaggerated indifference with Butcher leaving last because he had fetched a bicycle spoke from a box in the corner of the room. That was the reason for his name. He had never missed.

The street they took was crooked and buckled as bad as the corrugated iron fences they passed on the side and Tsotsi led them a way that was sharp with stones, and eyes, and dog's teeth. It was dusty and the end of a day, but still light, when they left the room. It had been hot as well, it being that time of the year, and the township was heavy that moment of their moving, with hope for the dark clouds in the east and thoughts about a wet world. It was a moment of respite, a slow moment between the long day and the lot done and the lot more to come with the longer night, and the township wore that hour the way a beggar wears his rags, the cast-offs of a better time, accepted but without gratitude, worn without pride. Children were despondent because there were no more games to play, busy women found themselves with empty hands, dogs stood around on awkward legs, old men dozing in the sun felt the sun go and awoke to find their bodies cold. It was an hour of despondent attitudes, when you kicked the dust if you had played in it all day, or stood up and spat into it if you had slept there in the sun. And having kicked you just stood, or having stood just waited, like the women with their idle hands, and tried not to see yourself in the other postures of uselessness.

But the moment of *their* passing, the four of them walking down the street with a purpose, was also the passing of that moment of respite, and more than respite, a moment of reckoning it had also been, when neighbour missed neighbour because the slum clearance men had been at work in that area and a few more roofs were down and the walls, without doors and windows, gaped like skulls in the fading light and you could still see the dust settling inside while you remembered the disbelief, the angry impotence, the confusion in the faces that had followed the cart loaded high with the sticks of furniture; a reckoning also for the old man who was prompted by the cold in his bones to count the days past and hope for tomorrow; a reckoning for the women who balanced the little money their men would bring home against their many needs, spending at the same time a meagre portion of hope on their safe return because this day had been Friday and ahead was the night and the four men passing that moment were harbingers of the night, that moment gone now because *they* had passed and rooms were suddenly grey and cold and mothers calling their children off the streets where shadows were running like rats after the four pipers.

And Tsotsi knew it. Knowing it not only as a fact as big as the brave men who stepped aside to let him pass, and the shopkeeper who hurried out to board up his windows and bolt his door, or as small as fatherless children and the whispers of hate that scuttled away down the alleys, he knew it also as his meaning. Life had taught him no other. His knowledge was without any edge of enjoyment. It was simply the way it should be, feeling in this the way other men feel when they see the sun in the morning. The big men, the brave ones, stood down because of him, the fear was of him, the hate was for him. It was all there because of him. He knew he *was*. He knew he was there, at that moment, leading the others to take one on the trains.

That is why in his passing down the crooked street, men looked the other way and women wept into the dust.

His name was Gumboot Dhlamini and he had been chosen. But he never knew until it was too late. They gave him no warning.

Gumboot was a man. Measured in hope he stood in his shoes tall amongst men, but even barefoot on a day back with an empty belly and a chesty laugh sounding the vastness of his humour as he walked into the city so that those who heard him looked up and laughed at him, even then Gumboot had stood as high as a head in heaven.

'Maxulu,' he had said a thousand miles away, standing on the side of the road with his wife, 'Maxulu, I will be back.' The white man had pointed along the road to Sabata's place as the way to the Golden City, so he started walking that way. His wife stood and watched him for a long time and later when she got tired, because she was heavy with child, she sat down on the grass and he saw her like that until the road took him over the hill, and he remembered her like that ever since.

He had also asked the white man how many days it would take and the white man had said he reached the city travelling in two days in his motorcar, which of course was faster than walking. Anyway, he started counting and when he reached ten and could count no further he made a notch in his stick. Thereafter he made a notch in his stick every time he had counted another ten. There were quite a few notches in his stick when he broke it killing the snake and had to throw it away. So he stopped counting.

The weather had been warm when he left his wife on the side of the road, and his belly full, but with time the nights grew colder, his one blanket thinner and there were days of hunger. He worked once and with the money he earned bought himself a pair of shoes which he carried wrapped up in his blanket. He lived through days of vast silence, tramping along the road with the unending veld stretching away unseen on every side, tramping through the clouds of dust left by the hurrying cars, always silent, very alone, but never without hope. Then on a big day of the new world he was in, the brown, flat, unbroken world he had walked into, on a certain big day, topping a rise he saw the buildings of the Golden City in a purple distance. And they were big, and that day Gumboot found his voice, and laughed, and hoped high again, and put on his shoes for the last day of his long walk.

In the city he found work on the mines and a room in one of the townships, and for a year he had been travelling from the one to the other in the early morning, with a multitude of others on the crowded trains, to work, and back in the evening, with the same multitude on the same trains, to sleep. He travelled safe for a year because he heeded the advice of others, and in that same year he worked hard and earned well and wore through the new shoes he had bought on the road, and had them mended, then wore through them again and then through them again and bought a new pair.

In some ways the year was a short one, and in others it was long, especially when he remembered Maxulu sitting on the side of the road and he got him a man who could make words to do him a letter back home. And now at last the year was almost over. In a week, only one more week of early steaming mornings and work under the ground, he would be going back with the money he had saved. Maxulu would be getting back her man very much the same as he had left, with his laugh still big, and his hands that were generous in the gestures of love and even in shoes, still as high as hope.

But Gumboot was a man and that has a second meaning. It has to do with death and the frailty of even those earthen cups that hold passionate draughts of laughter, that can be broken and all the life of a man spilt in the dust. Gumboot was this man also, in this meaning, because on that Friday night train going back to the township, a week before going home, Butcher was behind him and Butcher knew with unfailing accuracy the position of the heart.

Gumboot had made three mistakes. Firstly, he smiled. It was because of the long queue at the station entrance, you see, because it was only a week to going home and ahead of him was a weekend of no work and a man coming round to his room to write Maxulu the letter that he was coming back – it was because of the people, his people (there were so many of his people!): the smell of these other men, their impatience to be home, some sad, most happy; it was because of all this that he smiled and Tsotsi noticed him because that smile was as white as light.

His second mistake was the tie. Flaming red it was, with bolts of silver lightning playing on his chest, like those sunset storms he had seen as a boy when he had stopped on the long trek home with the cattle after a day in the mountain pastures, stopping under the torn and brooding sky to shout his exultation to the world and hear it echoing down the long valleys and then to run with fear when the sky answered and lightning struck deep in the mountains. He had bought the tie at lunchtime from the Indian hawker who trundled his cart of scarves and beads and bangles and bright things to the mine gate every Friday, bought simply because he had never had one and it would surely impress Maxulu. But it was a bright tie and made it easy for Tsotsi to follow him at a distance as the queue shuffled on its thousand legs, like a millipede, to the ticket office.

And there, the third mistake. He bought the ticket with money from his pay packet. In the moment and its exuberance he had forgotten a cardinal piece of advice for getting home safe on the Friday evening train . . . don't let anyone see your money. Why after all remember the silly warning when thousands of his own people stood around him, who like him were honest men and about their own business of getting home safely and quickly. One whole year and never any trouble on the 5.49 (always ten minutes late) . . . and so he forgot to slip a small coin apart when they had paid him, and instead now tore his pay packet open in a hurry, because the others behind him were in a hurry, because of their laughter and curses, tearing the pay packet open to find a small coin among the notes.

He hurried to the platform and waited there. See! He was still alive! But Tsotsi was closing in on his man, and when the train, the 5.49 (always ten minutes late), pulled into the station and the crowd surged for the doors, he used that moment to close in on his man.

And now in the train (still alive!), jammed in with as many as the coach could hold, going home in a smell of hard work and tobacco smoke, his ears as full as his nose with the low murmur of tired voices, himself impatient because the writing man was coming to his room at six-thirty and there was still a half-hour walk from the station, and in between all this thinking of Maxulu, then his tie, and seeing it crumpled by the rush to get in, wanting to straighten it but finding with slow surprise that he could not move either arm.

He never had time to register the full meaning of that moment. He tried a second time, but Die Aap was strong.

Tsotsi smiled at the growing bewilderment on the big bastard's face, waiting for and catching the explosion of darkness in the eyes as Butcher worked the spoke up and into his heart. Even as that was happening, Tsotsi bent close to the dying man and in his ear whispered a obscene reference to his mother. A moment of hate at the last, he had learnt, disfigured the face in death.

Die Aap still had his arms locked around the man's waist. As the body slumped the other three crowded in and with the combined pressure of their bodies held it erect ... a move unnoticed in the crowded coach. Boston who was nearest, and who was also sick, sick right through his brain, through his heart into his stomach, and was fighting to keep it down, Boston it was who slipped his hand into the pocket and took out the pay packet.

When the train pulled into the station the crowd made a second surge for the door, as happened every night, and the few on the station who wanted to go further up the line battled their way against the flood to get into the coaches, as also happened every night, but the 5.49 (ten minutes late) did not pull away, as happened occasionally on Friday nights, because those left behind in the coach and the few who got in found Gumboot Dhlamini and saw the end of the bicycle spoke.

2

'Okay. Okay! I was sick. What's that prove! Tell me. What's that prove?'

Butcher laughed. 'Ja. Sick man. Like a dog. Sick like a dog.'

'So what's it prove?' Boston spoke with vehemence, raising his voice above the laughter. He was losing control. Spit bubbles had formed in the cracks at the side of his mouth. He repeated his question and then the fifth person in the room, a woman seemingly asleep on a chair in the corner, looked up.

They were drinking at Soekie's place. There were many places to drink in the township, and their number and location was never quite constant from day to day, because the police were busy most nights and every day somebody new would get a bottle and set up shop. The choice was big. You could drink with the men or you could drink with the girls. You could drink alone if it was that sort of day and that sort of world, you could sit down on a chair in a corner and drag out the one tot to last all night and no one would give a damn one way or another why your mother was dead or your woman gone. You could drink with a picture on the wall or no picture at all. You could drink comfortable in a club easy, or sitting on a wooden bench, you could even drink standing up in a backyard.

Soekie's place had a table with chairs around it, and a few more along the walls, which were bare. There was a piece of linoleum on the floor but that counted for nothing because the floorboards were rotten. The light hung naked above the table and on nights when the wind blew and found its way through the broken window pane and the gap under the door, then the bulb swung slowly to and fro and the shadow of its filament moved in a sinister manner on the wall. There was one door in from the street and in the opposite wall a second door which led to the second room where Soekie lived, and slept, and ate her meals and played her gramophone and had her bottles hidden.

Tsotsi was sitting at the head of the table, rocking on the back legs of his chair. Die Aap was on his right, Butcher opposite him. The chair on his left was empty. Boston had not yet sat down. The woman was sitting apart in a corner. She had been there when they came in. She might have been there all day, with her head slumped forward, legs outstretched, her arms swinging loose at her sides, a meaningless mumble on her lips at odd moments.

Boston was wide-eyed, with spit on his lips.

'So what does it prove?' he asked.

The woman looked up suddenly. 'Come here Johnny,' she cried. She was in her thirties and spoke without opening her eyes. Her features were as puffy as well-kneaded dough. None of the four even looked at her.

· 13 ·

Boston's eyes were moving with nervous frequency from Butcher, to Die Aap, to Tsotsi and back again, moving as the moment progressed and the laugh developed again and the smiles stayed smeared, moving like a cornered animal trapped in a ring of ridicule, looking for its opening and its escape.

'Don't be so hard Johnny.' It was the woman again. 'Come and give me a kiss.'

Boston went up to her. She cringed. With great deliberation and a flat hand he slapped her in the face. Then a second time. Her voice dropped to a soft, vibrant register. She kept her eyes closed, but the frown went from between her brows.

'Darling. Darling! ! Come again Johnny.'

Butcher laughed. 'Not too much hey. Your maag can't take it.'

Die Aap joined Butcher in laughter. ' 's goed Butcher boy, 's goed.'

Boston gave up the struggle. He went to the table and emptied his glass, but still didn't sit. He suddenly seemed to have lost interest in the other three. He walked aimlessly around the room and at times opened his mouth as if something were going to come out, but when nothing did, he shook his head and carried on walking.

Butcher's glass was empty. He thumped the table. 'Soekie. I'm dry. You're slow tonight. Soekie!'

She answered from her room.

He twitched his shoulders. He was beginning to look at the woman in the corner, staring at her intently for a few seconds, then turning back to the table and fiddling with his glass, his hands noticeably more nervous after he had looked back at the woman in the corner for the third time.

'Soekie!'

'I'm coming for Gawd's sake.'

Tsotsi rocked gently on his chair. He saw it all: Butcher and the woman, Die Aap half asleep, Boston prowling the room, looking for some inward thing, some word that would explain away, or even just explain, that moment after the job on the train when he had sat down in the gutter and vomited, and more than vomited because Tsotsi also heard the sobs that slobbered out with the bread and beer of their meal an hour earlier.

Going to Soekie's Tsotsi had said to himself, I will do exactly the same as I always do. It was that simple. So he rocked in his chair, he kept his hands idle on his knees, he drank two drinks to their four, he watched them, he heard them sometimes and sometimes closed his mind and thought about nothing, and he said to himself repeatedly, It is exactly the same as always. He was persistent in this assurance and pursuit of an outward reality that was the same as always because, for some time now, in a strange way, it had no longer *felt* the same.

Boston had something to do with it. He hated Boston. That was why he had chosen to take one on the trains, because of Boston. Boston had been with them six months now. It had been all right before him. But when Boston came, it had begun, and Tsotsi knew why. It was because of his questions.

'What's your name Tsotsi . . . your real name?' he asked once, on one of the first days when he joined them.

Tsotsi gave him a chance, looking at Die Aap first before walking away. Die Aap knew why Tsotsi had looked at him, so when he was gone Die Aap told Boston how much Tsotsi hated questions about himself and how no one knew anything about him except that he was the hardest, the quickest, the cleverest that had ever been and that once somebody had tried to find out something and he was dead.

So Boston stopped asking questions, while he was sober, that is. He drank a lot, especially after jobs, and even then at first he hadn't actually asked them. But they were there and Tsotsi could see them, behind the blinking eyes that needed glasses, eyes that struggled hard to focus on him, and studied him until too much had been drunk and they turned away, or inwards, or closed for sleep.

His mistake was that he let this continue. A bigger mistake was to start playing the game with Boston, which he did when he began choosing jobs because of the other man, the ones Boston couldn't do, or hated, or made him sick. Because when Tsotsi did this, and Boston saw it, and made Tsotsi realize that he saw it, then Boston ventured tentatively from silence to the spoken word. That was the stage their play had reached that night at Soekie's, when Butcher had called for more liquor and Die Aap was half asleep, and Boston prowled the room and Tsotsi rocked on his chair, outwardly calm, the same as always, inwardly uneasy as he watched the blurred shadow of Boston through his low eyes.

Soekie brought a bottle to the table. She was a coloured woman in her fifties and her story was that she had been born in the best bed, in the biggest house of the best European suburb in the city, but her mother never loved her and that was why she lived in the township. 'I wrote regular,' she always said at the end of her story. 'I've got the address, but I get no replyings.' What do you write

Soekie, they asked her. 'My birthday,' she said. 'I want to know my birthday.'

And so Soekie was at the table with a bottle, collecting her money before pouring a tot into each of the four glasses. She hesitated a moment and then found something to say. 'Remember this is a clean place.'

On her way back she stopped at the woman in the corner. 'Rosie. Rose!' she said. 'You must go home man.'

The woman opened her eyes. 'Soekie my friend. My only friend ...'

'No man,' Soekie cut in. 'You must go. Nothing more.'

Rosie started crying, so Soekie left her and went into her room.

Boston, who up to then had not stopped his aimless drift around the room, came to the table and, resting his two hands on it, hissed out the word 'decency!'

'What's that?' It was Butcher speaking, a spasmodic, twitching Butcher who had been staring at the woman for a long time. He turned to Boston with impatience. He had no time left for him.

'That's why I got sick!'

'You was as sick as a dog man.'

'Decency.'

'What the hell is that?'

'Everything you are not.'

'Shit.'

'Ja shit,' echoed Die Aap who had stirred out of his half-sleep for the drink in his glass.

But Boston was no longer interested in them. Free at last of their ridicule, the very real meaning of his nausea, his collapse as Tsotsi had anticipated after a simple Friday night job (a big bastard who smiled too much, now no more), this meaning and his feelings, feeling no longer the need for defence, possessed him and pushed him down into the seat beside Tsotsi, at whom he was looking.

'You know the word Tsotsi?'

'What word?'

'Decency.'

Tsotsi opened his eyes wide and looked back at Boston. It was a red-eyed Boston. A wet-lipped, very serious Boston with his chin weighed down by his breath so that you could see his pink gums between his teeth and behind that his pinker tongue. That makes his words, Tsotsi thought, and a second later, he wants to hurt me. Books and words! I wipe my backside with books and words.

'Don't know it man,' he said aloud.

'You wouldn't.'

'So tell me man. Tell a man that word.'

'Decency.'

'Ja. That's the word man!'

'It's why I was sick Tsotsi.'

'What's it? Sickness?'

'Ja. That's it.' And Boston closed his eyes tight and sort of laughed with a mirthless glee. 'I had a little bit of it so I was sick and that big bastard had a lot so he's dead. Man, was he dead.'

'Go see a doctor Boston.'

'Soekie.' It was Butcher, who had emptied his glass with one swallow.

'Listen Tsotsi. I'm going to be serious.' Boston leant forward to emphasize his words.

'Soekie.'

'We've never had a good talk Tsotsi.'

'Go to hell man.'

'No listen ...'

'You talk too much man.'

'Soekie!'

'For Christ's sake man Butcher. Go fetch it yourself. I'm trying to talk serious.'

'You was as sick as a dog.'

' 's goed Butcher boy, 's goed.'

'Listen Tsotsi. How old are you?'

– And here there was a pause and dangerous lights in Tsotsi's eyes, so he looked away from Boston, first up to the ceiling as if he were seeing it for the first time, and then to the wall opposite, and the woman in the corner, travelling irrationally from thing to thing until by accident he found Boston's face in front of him again.

Tsotsi hated the questions for a profound but simple reason. He didn't know the answers ... neither his name, nor his age, nor any of the other answers that men assemble and shape into the semblance of a life. His memory went back vaguely to a group of young boys scavenging the township for scraps needed to keep alive. Before that a few vague, moody memories, a police chase and finding himself alone. Tsotsi didn't know because he had never been told, and if he had once known he no longer remembered, and his not knowing himself had a deeper meaning than his name and his age. His own eyes in front of a mirror had not been able to put together the eyes, and the nose, and the mouth and the chin, and make a man with a meaning. His own features in his own eyes had been as meaningless as a handful of stones picked up at random in the street outside his room. He allowed himself no thought of himself, he remembered no yesterdays, and tomorrow existed only when it was the present, living moment. He was as old as that moment, and his name was the name, in a way, of all men.

He looked at Boston and Boston looked at him, and Tsotsi felt a palpable movement in his stomach and a lightness in his heart.

'What's it to you Boston?'

And Boston who was drunk and deaf to the new sound in Tsotsi's voice pressed on regardless. 'I'm older than you Tsotsi. Ja man. Older by a good few years.'

'So what's that to me?'

'A reason to listen.'

'To you?'

'Yes. You know what I wanted to be when I was your age, Tsotsi?'

'I don't know. I don't want to know about you.'

'A teacher. I studied. I titcha-boy Tsotsi. I wore a tie. Ja man, with dots and stripes, like that big one tonight. That's what I'm getting at. That big one tonight. It's because of my decency.'

'Your sickness.'

'Ja, that's why I was sick.'

'Go see a doctor Boston.'

'Jesus Christ!' ... and there was no blasphemy in Boston when he said that. But Soekie was back with the bottle again and filled their glasses and also passed Butcher a 'cigarette' so that just in time the acrid smoke of dagga filled the room and Boston's wet eyes went unnoticed.

Soekie tried to move Rosie a second time. 'Rosie man. Jy moet loop.'

'Soekie my friend.'

'Nothing more man. Move.' She got as far as her hands under Rosie's arms when Butcher stopped her.

'Leave her.'

'For heaven's sake why.'

'Leave her!'

'You?' She looked from the woman to Butcher and back to the woman again. 'She was my friend.' But she shrugged her shoulders. 'This is a clean place hey. No rough stuff.'

'Leave her!'

Soekie went back into her room, leaving the four at the table and the woman alone in the corner.

Tsotsi rocked gently on his chair. Boston asked no more questions, brooding into his glass while the zol passed between Butcher and Die Aap. They took sharp, deep drags, smoking with a quiet intensity until their pupils had shrunk to pinpoints, giving their eyes a visionary quality, as if focused on some eventuality remote from the world they found themselves in.

When at last the cigarette was finished and his heart was so light it seemed to lie in his mouth, and the nerves in his groin were tight and his legs watery with desire, then Butcher stood up and went to the woman in the corner. He stood there beside her a long time, and so rich was the smell of his presence that as a reflex the woman moved in her seat and parted her knees. Butcher put his hand under her dress.

'Come again darling,' she murmured. He moved his hand higher. She opened her eyes. 'Not in here. Please. Not in here.'

He pulled her to her feet and pushed her to the door.

'Butchers Boy,' Die Aap said.

Butcher turned and looked at him. He shrugged his shoulders indifferently. 'Come,' he said, and so the three went out into the night, leaving the other two alone, the room thick with smoke, a dog somewhere in the distance, and behind the wall where Soekie lived, her gramophone grinding out the broken shards of an old song.

They stayed that way, Boston deep in his decency, Tsotsi considering a sudden, irrational impulse that had come to jump up and run away somewhere, considering this while rocking on his chair, outwardly the same, as always, both of them staying that way while many minutes passed, until a cry from the night where the other two had taken the woman made Boston look up.

'Where they gone?' Boston asked. Tsotsi made no reply but looked at the empty chair in the corner. Boston followed his eyes.

'Hell,' he said, and a second later with the second scream, 'Hell and Jesus.'

'What's the matter. Sick again?'

'One's enough,' Boston said.

'One what?'

'You know. You chose him.'

'It's not the same.'

'What's the difference?'

'She'll live.'

Boston looked long at Tsotsi. Because it was all ache now, and dull, the edge worn off like Soekie's old song, because it was that way he could look a long while without stumbling on words. When he did speak it was slowly, as if he had trouble putting words together: 'You feel nothing?'

'Feel what?'

'The big one tonight?'

Tsotsi stared empty-eyed at Boston.

'That poor bitch out there.'

Tsotsi slipped a shrug of impatience off his shoulders.

'Feel what?' he asked.

'Nothing!'

'That's what you said.' When Boston's eyes brimmed with disbelief Tsotsi was angry. 'What do you mean, feel?' he asked.

Boston put his glass down carefully on the table. He pulled his chair in closer, then resting his arms on the table he looked up at Tsotsi, looking hard, blinking against the blindness of habit, trying hard to focus on the young man opposite him.

'Listen Tsotsi, I want to know. I really want to know. Feeling. How can I put it. Ja . . .' He put his hand into his pocket and brought out a knife. He pressed his thumb down and the blade shot out. Then with great deliberation, wetting his lips with his tongue, he pulled the blade lightly across one arm crooked before him on the table. It wasn't a deep cut but within a few seconds it began to sweat out its pain in drops of blood.

Boston smiled down at it and then at Tsotsi. 'I feel that,' he said.

'So would I.' Tsotsi had stopped rocking on his chair. He watched Boston coldly.

'Ja . . . now this is it Tsotsi. There is something inside me that is like that,' and he pointed at the cut in his arm. 'When we dropped that big one tonight it was like that inside me. I bled man. I'm telling you I bled.'

'Decency.'

'Call it what you like . . .'

'You called it that.'

'Ja I did, that's true. But listen Tsotsi, we're on to something bigger now. Bigger man. Tsotsi answer me this. Does that happen to you? Does anything, anywhere do that to you?'

Tsotsi didn't answer. He didn't even consider the question. What he knew was that he started hating Boston the way he had never hated him before, and that with the passing of a little time and some sound of Soekie's old song, the hate was deeper and stronger than he had ever known. It was a cold hate, utterly merciless, and because he knew he was going to do something about it, right then and there, he could meet Boston's eyes without flinching. Boston had gone further than he had ever ventured before. It wasn't just a name, or his age, or where he came from; now it was inside, right inside Tsotsi that he was carrying the light of his eyes, and that was a world in which no one, not even Tsotsi himself, had ventured.

'A woman Tsotsi.' Boston was speaking again. He waited a long time. 'Maybe you had a woman. Ja, that's right. And when she let you down, or she left you, it hurt inside. Hey?' He waited a longer time. 'Not one?' Boston put his thumb and forefinger to his eyes. They were hurting. There was sweat on his upper lip which he wiped away. 'Your folks Tsotsi. Your mother ... or father. Sister? Jesus! What about a dog?'

There was nothing left after that, so he was silent. He didn't move for a long time and Tsotsi sighed once and then looked down at his hands.

They stayed that way until the street cried, then laughter, and Soekie started her song again at the beginning, staying like that, Boston still, Tsotsi seemingly the same as always, the one in disbelief, the other at the explosive moment of action, and this moment precipitated when Boston whispered: 'You must have a soul Tsotsi. Everybody's got a soul. Every living human being has got a soul!'

Tsotsi stood up, as if to stretch, his arms above his head, the elbows straight but bent at the wrist and turning. He opened his mouth to yawn but instead a cry came out and with that he brought one of his arms down in a wide swinging arc, catching Boston full on the parted lips with his clenched fist.

Boston went down, but before he could move Tsotsi was over him, and this time with even more force, because he could aim. He broke his fist into his nose, and then his ear. Boston moaned softly, Tsotsi stood up and walked a few feet away, standing eventually with clenched fists almost flush against a blank wall. Boston still moaning, softly, rolled over on his stomach and raised himself on an arm. His words were blurred by the blood and broken teeth.

'You'll feel something one day. Ja Tsotsi. One day it's going to happen. And God help you that day, because when it comes you won't know what to do. You won't know what to do with that feeling.'

Tsotsi spun around and in a few quick steps was beside Boston again. With a kick at Boston's elbow he sent him sprawling. This time Boston cried, and a second, and a third, and a fourth time as Tsotsi went to work on him with his shoes, using the heel and the toe, using everything he had learnt about pain.

Soekie came through the door and for a time struggled to keep Tsotsi back. It was only when Die Aap and Butcher came back, and joined her, and Tsotsi realized that he could no longer get at the man, that he broke away from them and walked out into the night.

They rolled Boston over and whistled through their teeth.

= 3 =

He walked out of the shebeen and into the street where the sky was low with storm clouds which had at last rolled over the township and the street itself, slow with couples in the dark and people lounged around in gentle attitudes of waiting for the rain. He kept his back to the shebeen and the street before him, broad as a river it was with eddies of life on the corners and around the lamp-posts, and the sluggish drift on the pavements, walking through this without once looking back to the room where Butcher and Die Aap were whistling through their teeth and Soekie was telling them to take the unconscious man out of her place, all of this while her gramophone repeated unheeded the meaningless phrase of its last groove. Walking away, he passed somewhere the woman the two men had taken out earlier, returning now with wet thighs for the drink she had earned, but Tsotsi had no thought for her, or the others, seeing only Boston, hearing again his words.

He saw Boston at the moment when he had raised himself on the floor, and spoken. Seeing him like that, with the blood in his mouth and the strange look in his eyes. Tsotsi knew the others had pulled him off before he had finished. He wanted to work a long time on Boston. He had only started. He was not released from the torment of his hate.

He also heard him again, hearing the words, but without their meaning. In those final insensate moments when he went to work on Boston, his mind had taken up the words, and like dice rattled them out of sequence and shape, throwing them now, as he walked down the street, back into his ears:

> One day one day God help you that day
> one day you won't know what to do what to do.

They caught the rhythm of his walking:

> It will happen will happen will happen one day it will
>   happen
> God help you that day, one day, that day, one day.

He stopped, and with his hands on his ears, and his eyes shut, he rolled his head from side to side, but that didn't help because the sight of him, and his sound, was inside, right inside. Tsotsi looked around desperately. He was near a lamp-post, and underneath it crouched in a circle was a group of men dicing for money. When they saw him walking their way they stopped their game, looked at each other and then without a word pocketed their money and drifted away into the night.

In a house across the street a party was under way. Tsotsi stood still and tried to see it. The noise of it, the music and laughter and droning undertones of talk, big talk, small talk, love talk, or just the babble of a drunk, this and the light and the smoke from cigarettes was pouring out of the doors and windows, and these were thrown open to their widest as if for fear the walls could not contain it all.

At the moment that Tsotsi stood watching, two girls came running out of the door, hand in hand, laughing their way down the street, and a minute later a man in hot pursuit, a bottle in his hand, calling after them, drinking as he ran. Tsotsi had almost succeeded in 'seeing' all of this, when the man slipped and fell in the street, sprawled the way Boston had been on the floor when he first went down. The girls laughed somewhere and the man raised himself on one arm and called out to them, but Tsotsi didn't hear him, not even seeing him anymore, because that way he was even more like Boston, speaking through his blood. The image came back, and the words as well, and it was worse than before.

He closed his eyes and clenched his fists and walked again, down the street, heedless of the people he pushed aside and the curses that snapped at his heels like small dogs; opening his eyes in time to a quickened pace that carried him sly as a shadow past other doors, other windows where light and murmurs and occasional laughter also fell in the dust; past corrugated iron fences with their slogans of a better world where the wet paint of the slogans had run a time back leaving the words streaked as if with tears, but even his rhythm, or that of his heart, or any of the other rhythms around him in the night, dog barking, dog whining, the thin notes of a penny whistle climbing somewhere in the darkness, a baby born, a cry, all of these in some conspiracy of intention finding the metre and meaning of Boston's words:

> One day one day it will happen a feeling
> will happen one day and God help you that day one
> day that day

so that at the corner where the church stood, humbly, its cross affirming that God moved amongst men that night, there he threw back his head and ran. He ran like a man possessed, his feet pounding out the panic of that moment, and those who saw him coming their way stepped aside, and all who saw him stopped and watched him pass. 'Que!' they said. 'A mad one.' But they were not greatly surprised. There were many. In a few seconds he was at the end of the street and like a buck he leapt through the last of the light and into the darkness that ringed the township, marking its limits and the start of the no-man's land between it and the white suburb.

It was here that he finally broke the spell of Boston and his words. He pushed his body to its limit, working his legs and his lungs until his mind went blank and then keeping on; for a long time it must have been, because when he stopped and leaned against a lamp-post he was in a strange street, in a different place, and at first everything was spinning around his head while the blood pounded in his ears. He stayed there, holding onto the lamp-post, for some time, his eyes shut while he sucked in and swallowed air with a desperate sound. Soon he was breathing easier and the pounding was gone from his ears. When more time passed and he had still not seen Boston again, or heard him, then he knew he was safe. He opened his eyes. The lights of a car had swung into the street further down, and were coming towards him. Tsotsi left the lamp-post and slipped into the darkness. It could be the police. The white suburbs near the township were well patrolled.

He didn't stop again until a long time later when somewhere in the night a clock chimed an hour he didn't bother to count. Soon after leaving the lamp-post where he had rested, the rain had fallen. There wasn't much of it. For all he knew it might have missed the township where they would have gone to bed sighing and sweating and wondering why it came so close and then didn't come at all. Tsotsi heard the warning roll of thunder, vaulted, distant; he saw the lightning over the rooftops, sudden, very white, like a woman shaking her sheets at her back door, and then it came. First in a few heavy drops that rattled on the leaves of the trees he was passing and then as a drifting cloud of coolness, almost mist it was so light. Street lamps shrunk to glowing, golden monoliths spaced at mournful intervals down the street, and then a shining belt of blackness with the grass like powdered glass on each side. He lifted his chin and caught the feel of it on his face, and he was completely at peace for a moment.

He prowled the streets, turning irrationally on sudden impulses and not even asking himself why he had chosen one way and now another. Curtains on windows, dogs at the gates. The drifting rain was with him for a little time and then it poured and some of the clouds lumbered away silently overhead, leaving room for the moon. Rooftops, left wet by the rain, shone brilliant in the moonlight. It was suddenly a white world, a prismatic, polished, gleaming world of white surfaces; the streets, the moon-washed walls and rooftops almost a glacial white. This quality was caught by his ear as well. In the wet, soft, shrunken curled-up moments of the rain, there had been silence. But now with the rain gone, excited by the moonlight, the crickets had come back. It was a hard, leaping, crystal sound defining the small facets of that moment. They were busy in the hedges, under the stones in the gardens, in the trees, and the distant ones seemed to sound as distant echoes of those around them.

The clock struck somewhere, and all was silent for a moment as they listened, so Tsotsi stopped and also listened for a while to the dull, discordant toll but did not bother to count. Ahead of him was a grove of bluegum trees and because he was tired, suddenly very tired, he turned that way, meaning to rest.

When he reached the trees (there were about twenty), he slipped quietly to the middle and stood for a moment quite still, noticing for the first time that there was a slight breeze. The moonlight lay around him in pools, splashing over roots and dry leaves, mobile as quicksilver as the treetops moved gently and their shadows shifted on the ground. The wind was just a whisper among the leaves and branches creaked intermittently with dry, complaining sounds. Tsotsi drew in a deep breath. The air was damp and drenched with heavy scent of the bluegums. His eyes, opened wide, mirrored the cataracts of light splashing around him. He was content and stood like that a long time until his legs throbbed and he remembered he was tired.

He sat down with his back to a tree and no sooner was he comfortable than he regretted it, because immediately the image of Boston rose up before him. I shouldn't have stopped here, he thought. I should have kept on until I could go no more.

He was not that tired that he couldn't have stood up. The ache in his legs was no worse than a ten-day-old knife wound. He could have risen to his feet and carried on to another place, another destiny, because the stars were busy that night. But instead he chose to remain, and in remaining picked up the silken thread of the chances that were to lead him a strange way.

And so the image of Boston, considered, now that his violence was spent, without the madness of hate. Boston! He, Tsotsi, had himself picked Boston from the thousand lives adrift in the location streets. He had picked Boston because he had a virtue, just as Die Aap had a virtue, which was strength, inhuman strength, and Butcher with his virtue, which was the accuracy that had earned him his name, an accuracy as reliable as the edge of a good knife. Boston's virtue being that he was clever. He was a lot of other things as well. He was a coward, he was weak, he talked too much, he drank even more than he talked. But more important than anything else – he was clever. He could think. Boston had already proved himself, a hundred times over. In as many jobs his cleverness had engineered success. The little details that got you caught, these Boston thought about, in a panic of fear it was true, but he thought about them and that was all that mattered.

It was simple and it would have worked for a long time if it had only stayed like that. Where had it gone wrong? It had gone wrong because Boston started asking questions, even after he was warned. And Tsotsi had not known the answers.

When he thought of himself inwardly, Tsotsi thought of darkness. Inwardly there was darkness, something like the midnight hour, only more obscure. At night when he lay on his bed it was almost one continuum of obscurity, as dark without as within, the separation being his flesh. Sleep was the moment when it happened, when he merged and everything was black. He never dreamed. This did not disconcert him, provided he lived according to a set of tried and tested rules. He didn't know where they came from, but he had them, and if he failed to observe them trouble started.

The first rule was the rule of the working moment. That moment always came as a miracle, a sudden eruption of light as he opened his eyes, and sound as well as sensation, feeling and smelling; being born twenty years old with the smell of the womb in your nostrils and its darkness behind your back. It was a moment of great peril because the impact of the world around him, on his senses, was like a flood that threatened to tear him away from his moorings and cast him adrift on a new day as aimless as the others caught in the wanton tides of the location streets. It was at this moment that his first rule operated. It was simply that before anything else, eating, washing, pissing, he had to see to his knife.

It was a sheath-knife, the blade four inches long. The handle was made of wood and was kept in place by two copper studs, and he carried it in the back pocket of his trousers, and slept with it under his jacket which he rolled up and used as a pillow. He would take it out, in the room in the morning, and look at it. This meant testing the edge on the soft ball of the thumb, and if it couldn't shave off a thin wafer of skin, then sharpening it. He used a stone for this, which he kept in his room. Sharpening it was, as someone had once shown him, to spit on the stone and then to work the blade lightly backwards and forwards. And if it wasn't in need of sharpening, he would simply play with it for a few seconds, enjoying the security of it in his hand. He knew the knife, the feel of it was familiar, its purpose obvious, it was his and he knew how to use it. These thoughts were cast out like mooring ropes and tied him firmly to what he knew. Whatever the case might be, the blade dull or as keen as sight, when he put it away in his pocket and looked up, the day was his. He Tsotsi, knew himself and his dark purpose, and everything was all right. The knife was not only his weapon, but also a fetish, a talisman that conjured away bad spirits and established him securely in his life.

His second rule which operated from then on through every other moment of the day was never to disturb his inward darkness with the light of a thought about himself or the attempt at a memory. He was not only resigned to not knowing about himself, he didn't want to know anything. This was an instinctive caution in Tsotsi to leave well alone. It was also the hardest of all his rules, because of the independent and irrational nature of life. There was only a limited area that he controlled absolutely. The vaster regions of it operated regardless of him, sometimes running against his purpose. Sometimes something simple would catch a sense, something evocative of something in his past, the smell of wet newspaper did it, and it would stir and start associations charged with pain and mystery inside him. Once, feeling secure in his bed in his room, he had seen a spider working at its web in a corner of the ceiling and seeing this he had known a moment of acute terror – and had passed a night without sleep, almost hypnotized by the spider, too frightened to kill it. And all he knew was that the insect, inexplicably, had evoked terror, and that something frightened and very small had moved within him.

Sometimes these encounters with his past were of a more definite nature. Like the time he and Die Aap and Butcher were rolling dice near the station and Butcher nudged him and all three of them looked up. A policeman was walking down the road towards them, wheeling a bicycle with one hand, the other dragging by the jacket a man who was handcuffed. One policeman, one prisoner in a deserted street. Butcher had smiled, Die Aap might have laughed, while Tsotsi waited and watched. The policeman saw them, and he slowed down a little, then tightened his hold on the man and walked on to them.

The prisoner was young, maybe Tsotsi's age, but as thin as hunger can make a man, with those large shiny eyes that go with it. He had been beaten. There was a trickle of blood from his nose. Tsotsi watched him, vaguely uneasy at first, more so when the man saw him and his face lit up with recognition and he looked quickly at the policeman and smiled suddenly with a wild hope. Butcher nudged Tsotsi. 'Okay?' he asked.

But Tsotsi didn't answer. He was remembering the face – but in his memory it seemed younger and the body under the face was that of a boy, a child with knobbly knees and empty hands. There was a memory of boys scavenging the townships. Beyond that he had never gone.

When the policeman and his prisoner were abreast of them he still hadn't moved, or given the word to the others. They looked at him perplexed. The smile on the prisoner's face was going, he looked hard at Tsotsi, hoping very hard. Butcher nudged him, and he might have moved then, but the prisoner looked at him desperately as he paused and called him by a strange name. David, he said. Tsotsi looked away, picked up the dice and rolled them.

'David!' the man called. 'David!' Tsotsi looked away. 'It's me. Petah. David help me.' David, he called, all the way down the street.

But Tsotsi had closed his eyes. He heard it no more. He forgot it.

Right there and then. Knowing it was a voice from the past, he made himself forget. Under the bewildered gaze of Butcher and Die Aap he rattled the dice and played on. That incident, and the memories it had evoked, was the furthest Tsotsi had ever gone back into his past.

His third and final rule was really an extension of the second. It was the rule Boston had broken. Tsotsi tolerated no questions from another. It wasn't just that he was caught without answers. It went deeper than that. Those questions sounded the vast depths of his darkness, making it a tangible reality. To know nothing about yourself is to be constantly in danger of nothingness, those voids of non-being over which a man walks the tightrope of his life.

Tsotsi feared nothingness. He feared it because he believed in it. Even more than that, he *knew* with all the certainty of his being that behind the façade of life lurked nothing. Under men's prayers he had heard the deep silence of it; behind man's beauty he had seen it faceless and waiting; inside man himself, beyond the lights of his loves and his hopes, there too was nothing, a darkness like an enormous unending night that closed in when the fires burned low and out, leaving only ash as an epitaph to their passing warmth.

The problem of his life was to maintain himself, to affirm his existence in the face of this nullity. He achieved this through pain and fear, and through death. He knew no other way. When Gumboot died, and in those last few seconds before death had looked hard with hate and then fear at the young man who had chosen him, that moment Tsotsi had known he was alive. It was as simple as that.

Tsotsi still sat with his back to the three with these thoughts, or his equivalents of them, the personal spectres that carried their meaning, some visual, seen inwardly like the face of his first killing, others felt, like the twitch in the nerves of his groin when he had savoured the meaning of killing. These had been passing through his head for a long time and now he was tired. He was not good at thinking.

He stood up, determined to run again, to leave the trees. He was already moving when he heard the sound, so he stopped, slipped quietly into a shadow and waited.

What he had heard were footsteps, about ten at a time, coming at regular intervals as someone moved down the street, crossing the silent squares of grass on the pavement, and then the driveways to the garages with the sound of a shoe on cement. They were regular but rapid, the rhythm of hurry and fear, almost a run. When he heard them coming steadily closer, Tsotsi moved to one of the trees on the edge of the grove.

It was a young woman, a black woman, coming towards him in the night. She was wearing a long coat, unbuttoned, and underneath it he could see a white garment that could have been a petticoat. She carried a small parcel and she kept on looking back.

From his position under the tree Tsotsi recognized without hesitation the symptoms of fear. Nothing else moved a human being the same way. He had seen it often. She held her parcel as if it were her last hold on life itself. Even if their hands were empty, they would hold themselves, hand holding hand. She was nearer now and he could see that her parcel was a shoebox. Fear too, and fear alone, made you see a threat of danger in every shadow, which is how she was, her head turning constantly from side to side. But most of all fear made you hurry. She was caught in an ungainly rhythm between walking and running, almost tripping over her feet in her hurry. Once or twice, with a few steps quicker than the rest, it seemed as if she was about to break into a run, but each time something stopped her and she fell back into her stumbling lope.

Tsotsi watched her from under the trees. Without realizing it, his heart began to beat faster. It was almost perfect. The woman came towards him in the night, he didn't know her, he didn't hate, but he slipped slyly from tree to tree to the point where she would enter the grove. He didn't know what he was going to do but his fingers flexed at his side. His hands were ready.

She was opposite him now, having paused on her way to lean against a wall and shake her head. She crossed the street and walked into the grove of bluegum trees.

He caught her by one arm and swung her into the darkness, his hand cutting short the scream of terror that had fallen from her lips like splintering glass.

A second move forced her against a tree and there, with his body pressed against hers, a knee already between her legs and his hand still on her mouth, there he looked into her eyes. She struggled once but he held her firmly. She clutched her shoebox with even greater desperation.

For a few seconds neither moved. He studied her calmly, her eyes, her neck with the pulse of an artery under the warm skin, deliberating his next move while the warmth of her body crept into his and her breasts, full and firm, panicked under the weight of her chest.

Unknowingly he relaxed his grip. With a twist of her head she freed the corner of her mouth and screamed a second time, but before he could do anything his attention was torn away from her to the shoebox she carried. He released her and stepped back sharply.

She had stopped her scream and was staring now at the box with a horror deeper than her fear of him. With both hands she lifted it, and when nothing happened she held it up to him and for a second time he backed away. With a sudden movement she thrust it into his hands, and he held it clumsily. Tsotsi only had eyes for the box now, and ears too, neither seeing nor hearing the woman as she turned away and with a low sob ran back the way she had come, deep into the white night.

The lid had slipped off in the sudden impulse of her generosity. Tsotsi had found himself looking at a face that was small and black and older than anything he had ever seen in his life: it was lined and wrinkled with an age beyond years. The sound that had stopped him, and saved the woman, was the cry of a baby.

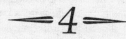

=4=

When he darkened the doorway, stepping out of the Saturday street and into the odorous world of Ramadoola, General Dealer, to stand quietly beside the bags of beans and mealiemeal, Cassim had had hopes of selling a few yards of one-and-eleven-penny printed calico to a woman.

'Flowers,' he had said. 'Pretty flowers,' and unrolled the bolt of gaudy material.

'How much?' she had asked.

'Cheap,' he said.

She fingered it.

'Feel it,' he said. 'Pretty flowers and it's going cheap.' They had kept that up for half an hour. There were variations, of course. Were the colours fast? They are as fast, Mama, as two-and-sixpence. Let me see two-and-sixpence. So Cassim took that bolt down – but in the end their attention reverted to the one-and-eleven-penny a yard. Half an hour was a good sign. He had hopes. Then his doorway had darkened and the young man was there, pretending he wasn't, standing beside the beans and the mealiemeal. Cassim looked quickly around the shop. There was himself and the woman he was serving and two other men whom his wife was serving at the other end of the shop. At that moment another woman with two children hanging onto her skirts came in. Eight people all together. That was enough.

'Pretty flowers, Mama,' he said, but he was looking at the young man. He didn't see the man, he saw the type. The slim, cool types of the street corners and the dice rings. The shebeen boys. The bad eggs. He liked that expression because bad eggs really were offensive to his thin, sensitive nostrils.

'Two yards,' the woman said.

Cassim sighed. He had hoped for three. He measured the material out on the yardstick nailed to the counter. He wrapped it up in brown paper. She paid. He gave her her change. When he looked again the young man had gone.

'Did you see that one?' he called out bravely to his wife, with a nod in the direction of the bags of mealiemeal and beans.

'God forgive us,' she said. She was a nervous woman.

That was at half-past-nine. At ten o'clock he was back again, standing at the same place, pretending he wasn't there. This time Cassim was frightened. There was only an old man in the shop buying a tickey plug of chew tobacco. He hurried around to his wife who was serving the old man. She looked at her husband with frightened eyes.

'Give him an extra inch,' Cassim said to her in Tamil. 'Talk to him.'

His wife cut off an extra inch and put it on the counter beside the tickey length. The old man shook his head and smiled. 'Tickey,' he said. He had a donkey cart and scoured the veld for firewood which he sold in the locations. Sometimes there was no wood.

'For you,' Cassim's wife said.

The old man, still smiling, held up the small coin to show it to her. 'Only tickey,' he said.

Cassim pushed his wife aside. 'It's a present, old man.'

'For me?'

'For you.'

'For what?'

'My respect,' Cassim said. 'My present, for my respect for you, being an old man.' Once started, Cassim couldn't stop. He explained that he had an old mother in India – living in New Delhi Street, Bombay. He told him about New Delhi Street – about India – he gave a short discourse on its history.

The old man listened without interrupting. He listened patiently, because that was the way of his kind. But inwardly he thought the Indian man was sorely mad. He was talking so much the sweat was on his forehead. What was he talking about? Why didn't he stop?

Cassim did, eventually. Somebody else came into the shop, and the young man left again – not once having moved from the bags of mealiemeal and beans.

Cassim called out to his wife, in a voice that was still a little bit brave: 'I fixed him.'

'God forgive us,' his wife said.

'What did he want?' Cassim asked aloud. 'Just standing there.' His wife was talking about Durban and going back. She had been born there. She always talked about Durban when times were bad or there was trouble.

'You know something,' Cassim said. 'I think he's mad.' He laughed. It was a brave attempt at a brave sound. That was eleven o'clock.

He came back again at eleven-thirty and this time there was nothing Cassim could do. They were alone.

His wife disappeared into the back room, where he heard her call all the children together. Then there was a series of door slams and business with keys as she retreated into the deepest room of the house. Cassim remained at the counter. He took a deep breath and waited. I can still scream, he thought. The young man came straight to the counter where Cassim stood with his eyes averted.

'Yes?' he asked, meaning to be calm and cool and to the point with no nonsense, young man, but his tongue had a lungful of air behind it with the result that he found himself saying yes for fully five seconds. He stopped in time to hear himself fart.

'It's wind you see,' he always said. 'A windy bowel.' At that moment neither the thought nor the explanation occurred to him. The young man was facing him and with prayers and inward tears Cassim was waiting for the first syllable of trouble.

'Yes yes yes yes yes yes yes ...'

'Milk.'

Cassim wanted to laugh. He almost collapsed under the hysterical desire to laugh. What sounds like milk, he thought. I've heard wrongly. Milk, bilk, kilk, schrilk, rilk, wilk . . .

'Milk.' A second time he said it, clear and strong and no mistakes.

Cassim looked up. 'Milk?'

Later in the day he found he could not remember the face, not even the clothes the young man had worn, because now when he looked his eyes, frightened and blind with fear, moved so fast from feature to feature that he saw nothing.

'Ja. Milk!' and this time there was anger and impatience, so much of both, so clear, that with an effort Cassim pulled himself together and found something else to say.

'But what sort of milk?'

'Baby Milk.'

'Yes yes yes . . . I see . . . baby milk,' and with another fart Cassim tore himself away from the counter, and disappeared, running through all the rooms and doors to the last, which was locked, and behind which his wife was cowering with her children. Cassim dropped to his knees and whispered, 'Baby milk!' But his wife, thinking that Cassim had just been knifed, started crying, and the children joined in. Without knowing it, they saved the day, because hearing them Cassim remembered, wiped away his tears and ran back to the shop.

The young man was still there, still alone.

'You mean condensed milk,' Cassim cried. He saw the young man hesitate and a frown pucker his eyebrows. I've got him, he thought. By God I've got him.

'Yes yes, you mean condensed milk,' and before the man could think enough to answer or argue, Cassim had the tin down from the shelf and on the counter.

'One-and-fourpence-halfpenny,' Cassim said, being careful to phrase his words as if it might just interest the other to know the price.

The young man was still hesitant, and made the mistake of picking up the tin and scrutinizing the label. He couldn't read and Cassim realized this.

'Very good baby milk.'

He paid Cassim, who gave him back the correct change, being very careful and correct, and he then left the shop.

Tsotsi stopped outside the shop. He stopped deliberately, forcing himself to do so, and looked at the tin of condensed milk, rolling it from hand to hand. I'm looking at it, he said to himself. I'm looking at this tin I've just bought. I don't give a damn about nobody. But he didn't see it. He was conscious of his back, and of Cassim's eyes behind it, watching him. For that matter he hadn't seen Cassim either, or his wife, or anything else in the shop. Buying baby milk – it hadn't sounded right. He hadn't heard anyone say a thing like that before. When he had paused long enough to prove that he didn't give a damn, he turned left on the pavement and walked his way and not once did he look back. He would have liked to run, to get away as quickly as possible from the shop and the two frustrating hours he had waited. Twice he had tried to just go in and ask. But each time he had got as far as two steps inside the door and no further. Buying baby milk! It didn't sound right. Two hours, until at last the shop was empty. Now he wanted to run, but again forcing himself, he kept walking.

At first he didn't see the street either. But C. Ramadoola, General Dealer, was a long way from his room. (He had chosen it for that reason.) And a few minutes after leaving the shop he felt better. No one was watching. No one was laughing. No one had pointed as he passed and shouted, 'Here's the man who bought the baby's milk!' He looked around and registered the time and place.

It was the Saturday street. The street had as many names as there were days in the week, as many as there were hours in a day. Saturday had one profound meaning. You had got past Friday. You were still alive. After this came the other meanings. You had money in your pocket. Tomorrow was Sunday, and that meant no work. You could live late today, and sleep late tomorrow. So you put on your best, you jingled your coins and you lounged about the corners watching the girls arm in arm flaunting their skirts the length of the street. That was the Saturday street. Lots of people, come today gone tomorrow, very hot, making up now for the banshee time around midnight when Saturday night would reach its climax.

Tsotsi saw it quickly and closed his mind to it. He had seen it before. Free of the embarrassment and humiliation he had felt in buying the milk, he was free now to hurry without a loss of pride. He slipped the tin into his coat pocket and pushed forward. People felt safe in the daylight and that made it harder to move through the crowds on the pavement. On Fridays they opened up and made a path for him.

When he reached his room he was sweating. He closed the door behind him, putting a chair against it so that no one could enter unexpectedly. The window, or rather the hole in the wall since there was no glass, he covered up with the thin square of wood which he used for that purpose when it was cold or raining and the wind blew. Only then, feeling safe from inquisitive eyes or interruption, did he take the shoebox from its hiding place under the bed. He put it down carefully on the table, pulled up a chair, sat down, and then took off the lid to examine its contents.

It was still alive and seemed to be sleeping. A foul, acrid smell rose up from the box, but he didn't notice it because for a moment he was again awed by what he saw. This was man. This small, almost ancient, very useless and abandoned thing was the beginning of a man. It had legs and arms, a head and a body, but even when he allowed for that, he still could not see how this would one day straighten out, smooth and shape into manhood. Even asleep its face was cross-grained with complaint. The head was misshapen. It looked more like an egg. The body was covered with patches of fuzzy hair.

When his first surprise was passed, Tsotsi noticed the smell. He left the table to fetch an old coat hanging on a nail behind the door, first bundling it up before putting it down. Then very carefully he took the baby out of the box and put it down on the coat. He was proud of that, the idea to use the coat. The baby looked better resting on it than it would have on the bare, bottle-stained table-top. Catching himself with the feeling of pride he frowned, pursed his lips and worked on. Apart from a stain on the bottom the box was still all right, which meant the smell was coming from the baby. He examined it. The smell was coming from its clothes, the rags in which it was wrapped.

Here Tsotsi hesitated. He sat down and wiped away the sweat which had formed a thin moustache on his upper lip. It was hard going. He hadn't done it before. What is more he didn't know what to do, and was forced to pause and formulate each new phase of action. The next phase had to do with the bad smell and dirty rags. The clothes had to be changed. How? He would use one of his shirts. Good!

He found one in the cardboard box in which he kept a few oddments of clothing. He began to unfold the rags in which the baby was wrapped. They consisted of a torn petticoat and an old pair of blue bloomers. This time Tsotsi registered a reaction. First distaste, because the smell drifted up on to his face as an almost tangible cloud of malodorousness. Then impatience and a sweat of panic when the baby awakened by all the movement began to cry. It was a shatteringly loud noise, and it made him uncertain of his hands. Finally he was surprised. He stopped what he was doing and looked down in amazement. The baby was a boy! The tiny penis rested like a thin finger on the testicles and these together were the size of a small walnut. The navel stood out prominently as a convoluted button of flesh. Tsotsi lifted up the baby and the origin of the smell was obvious. A crusty, egg-yellow liquid stool had soaked into the rags. Crumbs of it still stuck to the small buttocks. Using a corner of the petticoat, he wiped them clean.

When that was finished he wrapped it up in his shirt and put it back in the box, and the box on the bed, where he turned his back on it. There was still a lot to be done. He now took the tin of condensed milk out of his pocket, sat down at the table and examined it. Tsotsi had been seeing that tin, or others like it, for as long as he could remember, yet now as it rested on his hand it was as meaningless, with its label and words, as a book in a language foreign to his own, which he could neither read nor write and only half spoke.

Babies needed milk. Even he realized that. When he had got back to his room early that morning with the shoebox he had tried to give it water and bread soaked in water, but it had all come drivelling out. He knew what it wanted. Milk! And if the noise it made was anything to go by, it wanted it bad. So he had gone to the shop, but so uncertain was he of himself that it had taken two hours to find the courage and the right moment to ask. When the Indian gave him condensed milk he had wanted to argue. Condensed milk! He'd been drinking condensed milk his whole damn life. But the Indian had said it was baby's milk and had pointed at all the words on the label. Studying them now, Tsotsi found them totally without meaning – and apart from the words there was only the trademark picture of the two birds and the nest with the eggs in it which didn't help him at all.

He looked up at the baby. It was crying again, a hard, worrying noise that made him desperate and uncomfortable. He went to the bed and bending low over the puffed-up knob of a head shouted: 'Tula!' and then a second time, much louder, shaking the mattress with his hands. The baby cried on. If only Boston . . . No. It was too late now for that thought. He didn't finish it. Tsotsi looked once more at the tin, not at the words this time, just generally at the tin, feeling the weight of it in his hands and the noise of the baby in his ears, and then he decided.

'Right. You take it like I take it.' He spoke aloud.

With the decision he found himself busy again and that, together with the strong sound of the words, made him feel better. He made two holes in the side of the tin, using his knife, took a quick suck for himself, finding it thick and cloying in the throat, and then waited a few seconds while the viscous, white fluid slugged into a spoon. The baby took it and stopped crying. When the one spoon was finished he gave it another, and so on until ten had been slobbered up by the greedy lips.

After that the baby was quiet and Tsotsi took a rest. He took it standing up at the window, first taking down the piece of wood, and then resting there with his elbows sticking out. It was well into the afternoon now. He knew that if the others, meaning Butcher and Die Aap, were going to come to him for another job, it would be soon and if he wasn't careful he would be caught with the baby. He studied the street. It was the right time to do something. It was the Saturday afternoon lull, with most people indoors or sleeping or sipping away the hot hours until the time was long with shadows and the first rhythm of night began to trouble the blood. His problem was the baby in the box, in his room, where it couldn't stay.

Two men, the one with a guitar and an idle hand dropping warm chords as they talked, passed his window. Tsotsi had forged the first link in the reasoning out of his problem. He felt better. It must go some place else. That was even better. He felt good finding things a little clearer. Now where? Where could he take the shoebox? Soekie? Shit! She'd be just full of questions.

'Where man?'

'By Bluegumtrees.'

'By Bluegumtrees?'

'Ja man.'

'But why man?' – and how did he answer that. Ja, why? Himself asking himself now. Why? He turned and looked back at the baby.

No time for that now. The question was where. Where could he take it.

Tsotsi was still at the window, trying to think and finding it hard, when a group of men, laughing in their bare feet and dusty, khaki clothes, appeared at a corner and turned into the street. They were one of the demolition squads, busy each day now as they broke down doors and windows and tore off the roofs of a few more houses so that no more people would come into the township. They were being carted away in lorries to some other place, so that one day the township itself would be no more. Seeing them, Tsotsi had the solution to his problems.

The ruins, he would hide the baby in one of the ruins. There were already large areas of them in the township. They had been picked clean by scavenging children, but were now left alone, as ugly as ulcers on a weak body. Ja – a ruin. And the best one, because it was the biggest, began not far from his room, near the boundary of the impatient white suburb.

Tsotsi put his tin of condensed milk into his pocket, propping the holes first with bits of paper, then the spoon, and finally he turned to the baby. He replaced the lid, and picked up the box carefully so as not to disturb its sleep. He opened the door, looked around first and then stepped into the street, which was still deserted except for the dust of the men who had passed, a child without a game and a dog with a flea.

He asked no questions among the fallen walls. Neither why they were down and where had the people gone, nor was it right or what wrong had they done that it had come to this. He didn't need to. They had been asked. On that uncertain day, unremembered now because there had been so many like it, when the squad had come with sledge-hammers and crowbars in the first light, and the people had sat sleepy-eyed and bewildered on the pavement, that had been the moment of asking, voiced bitterly or inwardly, wordlessly, to be thrown away unanswered, as much the debris of that day as the rubble their homes had been reduced to after a few violent minutes of work.

Tsotsi passed through doorway to doorway, stepping lightly on walls that lay as they had fallen in the moment of submission. Those that still stood had been shocked into a dumb, gaping idiocy. Through them could be seen other ruins, and through those still others, giving a perspective of raw ends and rubble until it seemed that the space itself, the intangible something defined by four walls and a roof, had been broken up and holes knocked in it. Overhead the sky stretched as taut as a blue tarpaulin.

It was a good place to hide the baby. They were deserted, except for a few lizards grown bold in their undisturbed times. The people were gone, those who had lived there, been born there, gone away as much as those who had died there. The only ones who had returned, and then only briefly, were the children of the other families still in the township. They had come back for a short time starting when the demolition squad had left, returning to scavenge amongst the bricks, going home in the evening with wood from the broken doors and window frames, which had cooked simple meals in other backyards. They had come back another day, and maybe another after that to play there and lay the broken bricks in a child's dream of home, with a flower in a bottle and a one-legged doll. But they too forgot one day, because there were other games, other ruins, and this one had been picked clean. So the sun bleached the walls, the dust settled and the wind swept it clear of all smells of living. They were odourless as Tsotsi walked through.

He chose the old place where MaRhabatse had lived with her niece, and lived long, because the beer brewed in that backyard was famous. MaRhabatse had grown to a big age because when the time came to leave her room and climb on to the lorry she had hired to take her some place else, they found the door too small for the woman who in ten years had not left her room because of swollen ankles. The demolition men were forced to take the door away, and parts of the wall as well, before the big soul emerged to great cheering and many tears. Her passing down the street and into the distance, statuesque in her chair on the lorry, made real the whisper that one day the township would die.

Tsotsi chose this ruin because in one corner there remained an overhang of the corrugated iron that had been the roof, and he had thought about shade. The baby was still silent, so much so that he opened the lid to look, and was only satisfied when he saw the legs kick. He hid it in the corner together with the condensed milk and spoon, before sitting himself down, back to the wall, to think.

Tsotsi knew one thing very definitely now. Starting last night and maybe even before that, because sitting there with a quiet mind to the events of the past hours it seemed almost as if there might have been a beginning before the bluegum trees, but regardless of where or when, he had started doing things that did not fit into the pattern of his life. There was no doubt about this. The pattern was too simple, too clear, woven as it had been by his own hands, using his knife like a shuttle to carry the red thread of death and interlace it with others stained in equally sombre hues. The baby did not belong and certainly none of the actions that had been forced on him as a result of its presence, like buying baby milk, or feeding it or cleaning it or hiding it with more cunning and secrecy than other people hid what they had from him.

It had broken into his life with shattering improbability. It was irrelevant – and more than that, it was destructive, tearing open the simple hand-worked fabric in which he had wrapped his existence so that other irrelevances had begun to blow their cold way in. Why then had he taken the baby? – this being the time and the place for the question. The end of his logic was death, yet he had saved it. Why? Was there a chosen, a special death for it? He would have liked to believe this because together with the diligence of his clumsy, groping attempts to meet its needs, was resentment. Tsotsi squirmed with anger at the weak hold it had found on his life. Yet in spite of this he carried on, stumbling from one moment of inadequacy to the next, swallowing his pride, curbing his impatience, carrying on because he knew very well he had taken it. He was chancing his hand at a game he had never dared play and the baby was the dice, so to speak.

It was surprise that had made him step back, not yet twenty-four hours ago, when he had the woman under the tree. He had heard babies cry before, but remotely and without attention, hearing them as an off-key undertone in the bigger, bloodier sounds of life. But this one, coming then, the thin discordancies of it drifting up like stale smoke from the holes punched in the lid of the shoebox, those were so unexpected, so alien to his purpose and the meaning of that moment, that it had startled him. A lot was in the balance. The conspiracy of that night was almost hatched. The woman had brought it a step nearer fulfilment when she forced the box into his hands. The baby had taken it further still crying, because if it had stopped he would have surely heard the frightened footsteps receding in the night and that sound would have quickened him like a cat at play. But instead he held the box, heard only the baby, and felt it squirm inside, and inside himself a strange, nameless fear. The last detail in the plot was the lid falling off, because then he saw it, the hands adrift in the small boxed world like anemones in a dead sea, the head rolling from side to side, the mouth open like a black hole in its hideous grimace at life, the legs furtive and quick in their kicks as if it still felt the confines of its mother's womb. That moment the night was beyond repeal.

Suddenly, very sharply, and with more pain than he had ever felt before in his life, light stabbed his darkness and he remembered.

The memory was a dog, a bitch, a yellow bitch, and he knew definitely that it came crawling towards him, he thought possibly in great pain, but certainly crawling. There was at times even the sound of a whimper as she came crawling slowly, and as he thought, in great pain, crawling almost to him, very close, so that he could see her eyes, and in them the thought he had of pain. Then, just when it was certain that something was going to happen, the image blurred and faded and his darkness rolled in.

A yellow bitch crawling in pain ... that much he could remember, and with a clarity that even the innumerable times he had called it up since the trees had not faded by the slightest detail. A yellow bitch, crawling, in pain ... nothing had ever been as sharp in its effect on him, no pain, no pleasure, no event in the years since that certain moment when he had found himself alive and inwardly a darkness, keeping it that way until the bluegum trees when out of the past he knew nothing about, and had wanted to know nothing about, had come a yellow bitch, crawling, in great pain ...

Tsotsi looked up from his memory to find himself on his knees and before him, on the ground, where it must have slipped out of his hands, the baby still in the shoebox. It was much later then. The moon had risen overhead and was out of sight behind his back. The trees were silent because the wind had died away, and even the crickets threw out their triple syllables at intermittent wide intervals. It was still later when he left, because Tsotsi first of all had sat back to formulate. Something had happened that he had guarded against a long time. He had remembered. It was a strange memory. It was also ancient – going back further than he had even thought time itself went. The baby had brought it. That was also obvious and easy. The moment he had looked down, almost the exact moment of seeing it, he had remembered. The two were tied up together, somehow, the baby and the dog.

The next thought took a long time in coming – and when it did it frightened him. He was curious. This in its way was even stranger than the memory – because that had had predecessors in a half-bothered way, like the man who called himself Petah, and his fear of spiders and the nostalgia in the smell of wet newspapers. None had ever been as vivid, as terrifying as the memory of the bitch, but they did have to do with his past. But he had *never* been curious. Now he was. He knew his curiosity as a froth of futile questions that came to his lips. He wanted the answers, he wanted the answers very bad, but he did not have them. That was when he decided to take the baby. That was his talisman, his touchstone. It had worked once, working with devastating efficacy. It might work again. He would make it work again. He would wait until it worked again. His determination moved in the shadow of fear. Something urged him to kill the baby and leave it, warning him that he was playing a game he had never dared before. But Tsotsi was obsessed now, a longshot fool who had rolled the dice and had his first win, and then dared the lot because he wanted more. Tsotsi wanted to know everything.

So he carried the baby back through the wide streets and the dawn, passing under the first birds and their chatter in the trees, reaching the township at the same time as the sun. The baby would have to be alive to work its alchemy again. For that reason he fed it, and cleaned it and had now hidden it safely where he could return to it in his time and leisure, to lure the yellow bitch out of his past. When he left the ruins he had decided to return the next day to feed it again.

=5=

In the time that Tsotsi sat thinking in the ruins, two unimportant and unnoticed events took place in the township. Gumboot Dhlamini was buried and Boston awoke.

The cemetery was an acreage of crowded, sandy soil. There was a fence around the perimeter but termites had got into the poles and eaten them away at the base. Most of them now hung free of the ground, and a few had fallen over, dragging the wires down with them. The cemetery was really an accident. The people had had to bury their dead, and when the authorities came around to discussing the matter the cemetery already existed. It was then hurriedly made official, because with that strange reverence that authority has for dead bodies they sent in a team of workmen to erect the fence and to plant trees at regular intervals along its length.

The trees were a failure. They were meant to be cypresses but someone had made a mistake at the nursery. At least three-quarters had died, and the survivors had grown up deformed and twisted out of all resemblance to what was intended. They were a type of pipe with a deep, almost black-green foliage. If you took your sorrow to their shade you got covered all over the sticky, resinous secretion on the trunks and branches.

Gumboot had been allocated a plot near the centre. He was buried by the Reverend Henry Ransome of the Church of Christ the Redeemer in the township. The minister went through the ritual with certainty. He was disturbed, and he knew it and that made it worse. If only he had known the name of the man he was burying. This man, O Lord! What man? This one, this one here, fashioned in your likeness. What does it matter what his name was! This one. This Man. He had seen the face briefly when the police called him in. It was the hate, the hideous distorted hate of its grimace that he remembered now. This one, O Lord. This man fashioned in your image!

The other person at the graveside was Big Jacob, the digger. He had taken off his hat with respect and was resting on the spade. While the minister prayed, Big Jacob studied his head. It was the hair that fascinated him, very white and wispy, something like the seeds of a certain weed that drifted away under umbrellas of thin, silken threads. A wind was blowing now, ruffling the shock of hair, and he thought that if he waited long enough he might see it fly off. The Reverend Henry Ransome crossed himself and looked up at the sky with a frown.

Big Jacob looked down and played with the brow of his hat. 'Who is he?' he asked.

The minister looked at him once, very quickly, then back at the sky. He lifted his shoulders in a gesture of defeat. 'I don't know,' he said.

Big Jacob scratched his head before putting his hat back on.

'Friday night,' he said. 'We'll say we buried Friday night on Saturday afternoon.' Big Jacob began to push the soil into the grave. It wasn't necessary to shovel. It was all sand.

The minister turned and walked back to his church. He was sorely troubled.

Boston awoke and the first thing he saw was the little boy, standing quite still, watching him over the bicycle-wheel rim he was using as a hoop.

To be exact, it wasn't the first time he had opened his eyes since Die Aap and Butcher had carried him out of Soekie's and dumped him where he now found himself, in a back alley. Once in the early morning and again at noon, his eyelids had fluttered and opened and he had tried to get up. But pain had moved along every nerve in his body, and he had dropped back the few inches of his effort, unconscious. Now he tried again.

His head spun, a red mist drifted before his eyes, and he whimpered, but he managed to sit up. The child watched him, expressionless but intent. Boston looked down stupidly at his legs. Something was wrong. It took a few minutes before he realized what it was. Somebody had stolen his trousers, his good grey flannels, most probably while he was unconscious. A badly-torn khaki pair lay not far from him. The child was still watching, his chin now resting on the hoop. Boston opened his mouth but found he couldn't make intelligible sound. He gestured at the trousers, but the little boy ran away with a furious flurry of his short legs, playing his hoop in front of him with a short stick.

There was nothing for Boston to do but crawl across to the trousers. It took a long time and when he reached them he was crying. Every move had brought its own individual wave of pain. He rested, and then began the even more difficult, more excruciating job of getting the trousers on. The little boy came back with his hoop while he was busy, standing a safe distance away to watch him with the same expressionless intensity.

Boston staggered down the alleyway. Where am I going? he asked himself once. It doesn't matter, he thought. Nothing matters now. Not a single thing. He had seen his body and felt his face. He had remembered Tsotsi. There's nothing left. It's all finished now. At last. Every single bloody thing is finished. He felt like saying goodbye to the earth, and the sky, and the sun. If there had been a tree nearby he would have shaken its hand. He was convinced it was all utterly finished.

'He won't come,' Butcher said, bending forward to pick up a few stones, which he started throwing at a lamp-post.

'He will,' said Die Aap. They were lounging about on the pavement outside Tsotsi's room.

'Anyway, I don't care,' Butcher added.

'Same here,' said Die Aap.

This had been going on for a long time. The trouble was neither of them knew what to think about the fight at Soekie's last night, whether or not Tsotsi had included them in his attack on Boston. They had been discussing the matter ever since. Did it mean, for example, that the gang was finished or just Boston. He certainly was. He was more finished than anything they had ever seen. He was so finished he was almost dead. Soekie hadn't been able to help.

'I heard nothing I tell you. Just all of a sudden-like Boston cries.'

'What was Tsotsi doing?'

'Kicking him.'

'What's he say?'

'Who?'

'Tsotsi!'

'Nothing.'

'And Boston?'

'He was crying man, like I tell you.'

They hadn't worried much about it then because the day was finished, a job done, they had drunk a lot and taken a woman. Soon they would sleep. It emerged as a real problem the next day when they awoke. Time always posed the same question: What can I do with it? Your only escape from this predicament lay in a gang because that had a leader and he decided what to do. For a long time they had been following Tsotsi in this way. The prospect of getting through a whole day without him was unsettling. They discussed the matter, sitting in the morning sun.

'So what you say?' asked Butcher.

'He didn't say nothing to us,' said Die Aap.

'So?'

'So I don't know,' said Die Aap.

'He was finished all right.'

'Who?'

'Boston man!'

'Truly.'

'So do you think he wants us?' Butcher waited. 'Speak man!'

'I don't know,' said Die Aap unhappily, 'I tell you I don't know man.'

They drifted in this style through the day, through the streets, stopping for a drink, there for dice, somewhere else for something to eat, pulled on by gravity of habit and dependence so that around the middle of the afternoon, almost you might say by accident, since they were so free of a conscious purpose, they found themselves outside Tsotsi's room. They waited a long time, lounging around on the pavement.

'He won't come,' Butcher had said.

'He will.'

'Anyway I don't care.'

'Same here.'

Butcher was throwing his stones at the lamp-post. About every fourth found its mark with a dull, metallic note.

· 46 ·

'If he doesn't come I'll just go' ... clung! as a stone hit the lamp-post.

'I got places and people. I can go right now.' Clung clung. Die Aap had joined him in throwing stones at the lamp-post. 'And you?' Butcher asked.

'Same here,' said Die Aap. Clung.

Butcher dusted off his hands. He had had enough of throwing stones. He thinks he's good, but I can go. Clung. Die Aap was still throwing. 'Come let's go,' said Butcher.

'Okay.' Die Aap paused while he threw another stone. Clung.

Butcher had his cap so low over his eyes that when Die Aap nudged him he had to tilt back his head to see Tsotsi who had turned into the street a little way up and was walking towards them. They were both glad because one way or another the matter would be settled.

Tsotsi went into the room without saying a word to them. He ignored them quite simply because he himself did not know what he wanted. Butcher and Die Aap were in a strange way remote from his new realities. It was difficult to think about them, to decide purposefully if he wanted them or not. So what was he going to do? There they stood waiting for a word or a look from him. He was going to do nothing. Matters would take their own course. Something was sure to happen, and that would start something else and one way or another the problem would resolve itself.

So Butcher and Die Aap stood outside, looking at each other, and Tsotsi sat down on his bed in his room.

What happened was this. A young and comely woman, carrying her baby in a blanket on her back, walked past in the street. The baby cried and Butcher looked up and saw her. 'Feed him sister,' he called. 'Come feed him here beside me.'

The woman seeing him, and the lights in his eyes, spat into the dust and went on her way.

Tsotsi appeared at the door. He had heard Butcher's words and the baby. Encouraged by Tsotsi's interest, Butcher stepped away from the wall and called out to the back of the woman, 'If you got no milk, sister, let him suck me!' He turned to Tsotsi and smiled and said, 'Nyama,' which means meat.

Tsotsi was looking at this woman. There was a thought there. A big thought.

Butcher pulled his hat even lower over his eyes and walked up to Tsotsi. 'Shall we find one and play?' he asked.

Tsotsi shook his head. 'Later,' he said, and he was referring to the big thought Butcher's words had put into his mind. But by then the ice was broken. He had made contact with them again, so he said: 'Come,' and turned back inside. Butcher and Die Aap followed him happily.

When they had settled down at the table Butcher screwed up his nose and looked around the room. 'Jesus! what smells in here?' he asked.

Tsotsi said nothing, but went to a corner and rolled up the reeking swaddling clothes and threw them into the backyard where almost immediately a host of flies descended on them, and later a small and hungry dog dragged them away to a corner.

They missed Boston that afternoon. They missed his lot of words. Butcher tried his best, but told each of his four stories in a few words.

'Once I took a man on the trains and he had a hundred pounds.' What else was there to say about the matter. 'A hundred pounds.' Or the time of his escape. 'We killed him in the kwela-van. We jumped on him.' Boston would have gone on for ever with a sentence like that. 'The four of us did jump on him and kick him.'

When these two were told there was left only the time he had worked with Morgan 'Blackjack' Mogotso and the white woman whom he caught alone in the house. When those were also told, there was nothing left. They sat in silence and for a long time the only sound was the strange sucking noises Die Aap made when he put his big lips to a beer bottle.

Tsotsi surprised them both with his question. 'Where's Boston?' Die Aap blinked and Butcher opened his mouth but nothing came out. It wasn't the thought of Boston that surprised. He had been constantly but unvoiced in both their minds that afternoon. What surprised them was Tsotsi asking. He was looking at Butcher, waiting for him to speak.

'I don't know,' Butcher said.

Tsotsi closed his eyes and then looked into the street. Butcher fidgeted in his seat. He felt that capital should be made of the mention of Boston to keep the words flowing. But how? 'Maybe at Soekie's place,' he said. And then later: 'We left him there, at the back.' He struggled once more with the silence. 'He's bad. Wragtig bad hey,' and he looked at Die Aap, who took his lips away from the bottle, said 'Bad,' and then had another drink.

Then Butcher gave up. The few sparks of interest and word about Boston died away. Tsotsi closed the subject by ignoring it as abruptly as he had opened it, and that only because he was thinking about condensed milk. He had decided to forget about it when he left the ruin. I have fed it, I have hidden it safe, I will come back tomorrow, he had said to himself. In the meantime I will carry on as always. It hadn't worked that way. The thought about the shoebox and its contents, the enigma of his memory of that bitch, these slipped back repeatedly into his consciousness no matter how determinedly he had thrown them out a few minutes before.

The simplest things started the sequence. Butcher had teased a woman and before Tsotsi knew what was happening he stood at the door thinking about the baby. A little later Butcher had smelt the rags and back it was again. The baby, the shoebox, the bluegums, the bitch – over and over again, sometimes this cycle extending itself to include another detail like condensed milk – which is why he had asked about Boston.

Added to this was another problem which was much more elusive in Tsotsi's struggle. It started off quite simply as his awareness of Butcher and Die Aap. They were there. He had wondered if they would come and they had. He himself had taken them in, taken them back, so to speak. Why then did he find himself looking at them at odd moments with something like irritation and impatience. Theirs was a ponderous presence. In a subtle, ill-defined way it was in-trusive, almost an encumbrance. He had never been conscious of them like this before. In fact it had only rarely happened that he had been conscious of them at all, as the people with whom he lived and had to lead. Boston had been an exception. Boston through definite actions had made Tsotsi aware of him. The same thing had happened now to Butcher and Die Aap, yet they had done nothing.

Out of this vague drift of feeling and thought – the two men at the table alternating with the baby and the box and the bitch under the bluegum trees – emerged another problem, but this was as defined and decisive as the others were nebulous and vague. It was nearing the time when it was expected of him to announce the plan of action for the night, and he had nothing to say.

How had it worked the other times? Boston would be talking and they would be drinking and listening, only half hearing, adrift on the flow and sound of words, their eyes half closed except when groping for another bottle under the table or reflecting on the length of the shadows in the street, and by their length measuring the time between that moment and darkness; Boston telling his long, long story until somehow, something, some small thing like a thought, or a shadow, or a feeling, even a word, some small thing like that would precipitate in his inward darkness a desire, minute and murderous. That was the beginning, because with time it grew and became the purpose he finally spoke that led them out of the room and into the night.

That was how it happened. But now it was different and not happening at all, and it wasn't just because Boston wasn't there. What was expected of him, what the other two were waiting for, was a decision and this was something else that Tsotsi had never been aware of before. It involved choice. Was it to be the trains again, or a taxi driver, or a darkened, deserted house in one of the white suburbs. These, and their variations, were his repertoire, and they, Die Aap moody and Butcher twitching with impatience now, were waiting for him to choose.

It was the awareness of alternatives that disturbed Tsotsi and seemed to paralyse his will. Up to that moment he had lived his life as the victim of dark impulses. They had been ready, rising to his moments of need all through his life. Where they came from he never knew, and their reasons for coming he had never questioned. What he realized now was that something had tampered with the mechanism that had governed his life, inhibiting its function.

Tsotsi slammed a clenched fist into the palm of the other hand, and the other two, thinking he had decided, looked at him expectantly. He stood up and walked on stiff nervous legs to the door.

'What we do Tsotsi?' Butcher asked. 'Speak man.'

He closed his eyes and grabbed at his first thought. 'We go to the city,' he said.

This was hardly an answer because the city was big and going there could mean a taxi job, or prowling around for a dark house, or a drunk near one of the shebeens around the mine dumps. It was vague and an evasion but Tsotsi didn't care because the others, reacting to the purpose it suddenly gave to life, had stood up and were following him into the street.

Butcher looked back once at the room. 'Did you smell man?' he asked Die Aap. 'There's something smelling in there. Stinking like shit.'

=6=

When Tsotsi said 'city' he meant the open space formed by the junction of two streets near the gasworks. It was known officially as Terminal Place, but people referred to it variously as 'the shopping centre', because anything and everything could be bought in the small, dimly lit shops that were crowded along the sides, and from the hawkers' carts parked in the gutter, or 'the backyard', because of its relationship to the rest of the city, which was the white man's world. One wit had even referred to it as 'the quid-wrangle'. The sophisticated spoke simply of 'the beginning' or 'the end', depending on which way they were travelling, because it was here that the buses with their bone-rattled multitudes came together and parted on their endless traffic between the city and the townships.

A few blocks away, if you walked with your back to the massive cooling towers of the gasworks, was the 'real' city, the illuminated, glittering arcades of the white man's world. It might just as well have been on the other side of the earth. The life of Terminal Place, the shopping centre, the backyard, the beginning or the end of so much, this life started and stopped, faltered or was furious for its own intimate reasons.

It starts early in the morning, so early that in winter that hour is still part of the night. The first bus comes with its headlights on and its passengers blinking owlishly at the world through the cobwebs of sleep. These are the first workers and in the cold, steaming morning, breathing their ghosts, they walk away into the city, hands in their pockets, the collars of their jackets turned up and their shoulders hunched almost above their heads. A few of them have stayed behind to buy a tin of hot coffee and a vetkoek from the old woman on the corner. They stand around and drink gratefully and tear off chews of the doughy cake with their teeth. When they talk it is softly, the words thick with sleep and spoken at the back of the throat. Before they are finished the second wave of buses has pulled in and sent another tide of black men hurrying through the streets.

By the time it is light, Terminal Place is alive. The shops are opened, the hawkers have trundled up their carts and unpacked their wares, the pavements are bustling with women fat with pride and progeny, with men thin with poverty and persistence, and youth full of tease and tit. They bump each other, they buy from each other, bargaining, bantering all the time, they come together and part, friends are seen for the first time in many years, or for the last time in just as many years, many no longer look hopefully for the missing brother or husband or father. And through it all the buses still come and go. They travel urgently, jokingly, joltingly, tirelessly along the tentacled routes flung far and wide, tapering away from the compact body to the last stops in the dusty, rutted roads of the townships.

The life of the Place begins to decline in the late afternoon, the end starting when the windows, high and wide a few blocks away, burn gold with the last reflection of the setting sun. Night is near and night is never safe. The fluid life of the pavements slows, and thickens like porridge left too long on the fire. Windows are boarded up, doors are locked, the bus queues sag like slack ropes between the lamp-posts. The people go home. When it is finally empty, much later, much darker, the street sweepers drift through last of all, singing softly over the gentle rhythms of their brooms.

It was into Terminal Place, at half-past-six, when the last of the day had turned those high windows into angry eyes, that Tsotsi and the other two rattled and roared on the 6.10 special from the township.

He left it fifteen minutes later. He left it alone. He had lost the other two in the crowd. But he didn't care. He had found his victim and he had a feeling for taking him alone.

Morris Tshabalala was his name and he was also a man. But his stature, the extent of his manliness, was not in his body, because there was very little left of it since the accident, and what there was he dragged knee-high through the streets, using his arms like oars; nor was it in his hope, because there was even less of that. How then did he measure himself as a man? ... because he used that word, throwing it back at the children when they smiled, even though they had done so in pity, screaming it once at a prostitute who laughed at his money and desperation. Ask him and he will tell you. Bend down low where he sits on the fringe of the forest of legs rushing past on the pavement; better still, squat there so that he can look you straight in the eye. Don't smile, even in pity, don't try to bribe him with a penny, because only then will he give you the measure of his manhood.

'I tell anyman – *anyman* I tell you – I tell go to hell Mister! Go to hell and cook for your black sins!'

Whatever else you could say or see about him, Morris Tshabalala was not afraid. That is why, when the foot came down on his hand on the pavement of Terminal Place, he had no hesitation in saying in anger: 'Whelp of a yellow bitch!'

It wasn't because of the pain. His hands were hard now, his fingers had forgotten their disgust of the gobs of phlegm or dog piss because they no longer felt them. It was the insult of the foot that stung him. It meant he had been seen and nothing provoked so easily to life the harsh and bitter truth about himself. No one found half a man as meaningless as Morris Tshabalala himself.

'Whelp of a yellow bitch!' he cried when the foot came down. 'Can't you look where you go!'

Usually they shook their heads and stepped aside. Some even commiserated, calling him Little Father. 'Little Father,' they said, 'forgive me. But I did not see you' – which only made matters worse.

But this time it was different. The man said nothing and he didn't move, not even to smile or scowl. He simply remained standing in front of the cripple on the pavement. Finding his way still blocked, Morris Tshabalala threw back his head to swear again. But he didn't. He was moved to caution. Something in the eyes looking down at him, as remote as mountain peaks, as cold, as sheer with threat, made him keep his peace. He satisfied himself with a grunt, swung his body to the left and carried on his way.

It wasn't fear. Morris Tshabalala admitted to having known fear only once, and anything that did not add up to the terror of that moment was something else. It was the day the mineshaft collapsed. Day? There was no sun down there, and by the same token it was not night, because there was also no moon. It was altogether another world where time was a length of labour called a shift, and although the men changed, coming and going in helmeted gangs, the work never stopped, and the lights never went out, shining continuously on the damp, dripping sides of the shafts and the gleaming, sweat-wet bodies so that it seemed that everything was compounded of the same elemental stuff. A man was no more than a chunk of the earth that had torn itself away to hack and hammer and blast unceasingly at the body of his mother.

We are moles – they sang.
We are become rats.
The owl is my brother.
The sun is a stranger.
And does not know me.
The moon is a shy girl
And has hidden her face.
And dissatisfied wife
Has left my bed.

They heard it in silence because the lights had gone out suddenly and they had stopped singing and working and were standing quite still. They knew it for what it was. Above ground they spoke about it often and those who knew said it sounded like a rumble in the belly of a bull elephant.

'Gotso!' someone whispered. 'It has happened.' And then they had all run. Bedlam followed as they stumbled around in the dark, frantic and hysterical in their efforts to get away. If there had been light more might have survived. He might have escaped unscathed because when they eventually found him and lifted up the heavy beam that had fallen across his legs he was only a few yards from the spot where he had been working.

Am I getting old? he thought now. Does half a man get older quicker than a full one? Am I getting old that a child's eyes can silence me? 'Tsotsi,' he said aloud and spat onto the pavement. 'Tsotsi shit! Dogshit! Mangy, dug-dry, yellow bitch shit!'

Morris Tshabalala was on his way to the eating house where he always had his supper. He moved slowly through the crowd. He moved slowly normally but a lot of people made it worse. There were times when he had to wait minutes on end before sufficient room opened up for him to carry on. He moved by putting his hands down in front of him, the palms flat and then dragging his body forward between his arms. This position limited his gaze to the small area of ground immediately beneath his head and a little more on each side, because he could turn his head either way. If he wanted to look anywhere else he had to stop and sit upright with his stumps sticking out in front.

He was glad when he turned out of Terminal Place and into the deserted street. The paving stones were still warm under his calloused palms. This side of the street had had the sun from noon until a few minutes ago when it had disappeared behind the thick belt of smog that ringed the city.

Warm stones, he thought, I can still feel you, and I like to feel you. Anything that is warm I like to feel because once my legs went cold and I learnt that cold is the touch of death. Warm stones, how much longer will I feel you? My hands are dying on me because of the too much work in dragging me through the streets. Six years they have worked now. Yes, six years and already there are parts as hard as the hooves of oxen, and these parts no longer feel. That first year, the summer of the first year, the first day of that summer, when I left the hospital only half a man, then my hands felt everything. Ow! they felt the stones and the hot tar and the burning metal lids of the drains, and that night when I picked the grit and dirt out of the broken blisters and cuts, then I cried and asked myself was it not better that the coldness had gone beyond the hip, through my heart and into my head so that they had buried the lot of me. But then I found that butter soothed my hands and it was easier and the next day came and went and now here I am, many, many days later, and my hands are hard and only in some places do they still feel the warmth in these stones. I had a woman once, and when I fondled her breasts I felt the warmth of life.

He was halfway down the street when he stopped to rest. He examined his hands first, feeling one with the other, and the parts where his blackened nails made a hard, rasping sound on the callouses of too much work, feeling nothing in either. The silence was sweet, melting like butter on his sore thoughts. There were no reminders of the past or mirrors of the present. He looked back the way he had come.

A man was sitting on the doorstep of a shop a little way down, scratching disinterestedly on the pavement with a matchstick. Beyond him the chaos of Terminal Place was sorting itself out. The crowds were already much thinner since he had left. There was enough room now for the greasy pages of newspaper that had held a sixpence worth of chips to waltz between the legs. Occasional gusts of the same wind came scurrying up the gutter. Small clouds of grey dust billowed up and then fell back exhausted by the effort. Things like empty matchboxes or crumpled balls of paper moved suddenly and for no reason, skipping away across half of the street, to lie there, twitching furtively for a few seconds until another irrational impulse carried them off at a tangent to their first move. It was a warm wind. Morris Tshabalala felt it, screwing up his face each time a flurry of dust swept into it. He wiped away the grit that had collected in the corner of his eyes and then continued his journey. Once he started moving again, his face was even more exposed to the stinging clouds of dust, so he kept his eyes closed, opening them only occasionally to see that his path was clear.

Why do I go on? he asked himself. I am not better than a dog, and slower. Why do I go on? It was a recurring question in his life. It had many forms, each of them sounding in their own way some new depth in the seas of disbelief and bitterness that swept him away from other men into his present loneliness. Is that all of me? he had asked himself in hospital. It seemed so little he could easily imagine his legs jumping around some place else and calling themselves Morris Tshabalala. Another time he had asked himself: What is there to live for now? The beam that had fallen on his legs had also come down like a guillotine on his life, severing him from all the purposes, the plans, the places he had known as a full man. They were gone. Those that hadn't left of their own accord he had left, turning his back on them the day he escaped without permission from the hospital. He still did it occasionally when he saw a face he knew or seemed to remember, turning away and hiding his until the person was past.

Why does my heart not die for the shame of my life? When we chopped off the heads of fowls in my youth, the bodies ran around a little longer. It is like that with me, only it is my legs that are gone.

When he stopped again he was almost at the end of the street. He rested like a boatman hunched over his oars. A few yards away the rapids were whirling past on the pavements of the main street. A lot had happened since his last rest. The wind seemed to have wandered off and got lost. The day was finished. Around him the stones of the pavement, the street itself, the walls and the sky had merged in grey, ashen lines. Behind him the street lamps, alight now, walked back to Terminal Place. It was at last deserted. From time to time the dust and litter still rose and turned balletically before falling back like the last survivors of an orgy. It had been a busy day.

Much nearer Morris Tshabalala and sitting as he had sat earlier, on the doorstep of a shop, scratching disinterestedly on the pavement with a matchstick, was the same man. At first he did not pay him any attention. Then Morris realized there was something strange about his being there. For a few more seconds it eluded him. Then he found it. The man, sitting on the doorstep of the shop, scratching disinterestedly on the pavement, was roughly the same distance from him now as he had been four blocks lower down. He examined him with quickened interest. There was something else about him. He also found that after a few minutes. He was the one who had tramped on his hand in Terminal Place.

They remained like that, the cripple and the young man, a long while, and in that time Morris Tshabalala saw many things, like the slim arrogance of the body, the soft, idle hands and the head that pretended not to look but was doing so all the time. There was also time for other thoughts, like: Why did he choose me? and Tsotsi shit! and Has he been with me all day counting my money? Then he dragged himself as quickly as he could to the crowded and well-lit Main Street of the city.

The money, he thought. The money! I was right to despise it, because he wants it and if I am not careful he will kill me for it.

The money! But how else could I buy bread to eat and butter for my hands? Did I not try?

Yes you tried, Morris Tshabalala. On that first day of the summer six years ago you tried and said: Missus please. Even if it is just the weeds in your garden. But you could see that they were not really looking at you. They pretended to be staring hard at something else on the ground, but not at you, and you knew already what it meant.

When night came and you picked the dirt out of your blisters you were still without work. Having nothing else to do, you counted the pennies and few tickeys that had come your way and realized that there had been five shillings, starting with the old woman with the white hair and the fat dog; five shillings up to the last penny and who had that been? You hadn't even looked up to see, but thrown it away like the others.

The old woman with the white hair and the fat dog: 'John my poor boy!'

'Morris Medem.'

'Johnny poor boy, what happened to your legs?'

'Morris Medem. Morris Tshabalala.'

'Does it hurt?'

'Morris Tshabalala Medem is looking for work.'

'Stop it Biggles.'

'Work Medem.'

'Biggles *stop it*. Come here.'

'Anything Medem.'

'Oh these dogs!'

'Your garden Medem.'

'It is lovely.'

'I'll weed it Medem.'

'Good heavens! There are no weeds in my garden.'

Then she had gone and come back with the penny which she gave him, afterwards closing the door, and Morris Tshabalala, because he was looking for work, had thrown it away.

Not many had given it to him like that though, actually stooping down to drop the coin into his blistered palm. Most of them had simply fallen beside him out of the sky, falling hard and metallic like the first drops of a sky that has promised the miracle of real relief and then broken faith and blown away, and he for his part threw them all away because Morris Tshabalala was looking for work. Five shillings it had been, counted with deliberation and anger at the end of the day because it helped to pass the time. The next day it had been three shillings and five pence. It was more or less the same for the days that followed, rising once sharply to just under ten shillings because that day he had cried and there was no bush he could crawl into and hide his tears. The pennies had showered down. That was also the first day he kept the money, and it happened this way.

He had stopped with his sorrow and tears on a street corner. His hands were too sore to carry him any further, his heart too heavy to drag down another street in his fruitless search for work. The determination he had had when he left the hospital to survive as best he could was gone, and also his hope. Even his desire to survive. He had stopped on the corner, dragged himself into the doorway of an empty shop, out of the way of the hurrying feet, and for the first time that he could remember in many years there were tears in his eyes. So, not caring, he had just sat and let them come and the pennies had come falling down. He had not even cared enough to throw them away, because he was too tired in his heart for even that. Hours later, many hours later in the time between day and night, when the streets emptied and were silent and windy while the city waited for the moment to switch on its lights, then Morris Tshabalala had looked down and considered the money.

He was hungry and had spent the last of his money. He didn't have so much as a penny for a crust of bread. He had no work. He would get none. But he despised the money beside him. He despised it because of the way of giving and because he hadn't worked for it and the people who got money they hadn't worked for were of a different breed from Morris Tshabalala.

Ten shillings it was, mostly in pennies with a few tickeys and one sixpence. To be exact it was nine shillings and sixpence because when he had sorted it out, being a neat man, there were seven shilling lots of pennies, two lots of four tickeys each and one sixpence, all in a row before him. He realized he'd made a mistake in letting it accumulate. It was difficult to get rid of when there was so much. If he started throwing the pennies and tickeys and one sixpence into the street, it would attract attention even at that hour. They might think him mad or take him away or do something equally terrible. So what was he to do? Leave it? Yes. Right. Just leave it and not look back. Fine. He would go somewhere. Where? Somewhere. But where? Not the eating house because he didn't have any money for bread, let alone the butter for his hands.

Nine shillings and sixpence in pennies, tickeys and one sixpence. It wasn't a long struggle. Maybe half an hour later, so short it had been, he started down the street which was coming alive with lights and people, dragging himself and the extra weight of the despised money, despising himself for having taken it.

Once lost, that battle was never fought again. The next day he was back at that corner and the days after at others, some better, some worse, until he knew them all. The character of each he learnt was different, and their times too. There was one which he sometimes worked late at night to catch the crowds from the bioscopes. The same one was useless during the day, while the one near the market was only good for an early hour. Together with this there were other things he had to learn, like choosing one spot and sticking to it, no matter how bad it seemed to be. At first he sometimes wore himself out trying one place after another, and ending up with sore hands and little money.

When all this knowledge had been acquired, Morris Tshabalala never went hungry again and always had money for butter until his hands no longer needed it, so it went on his bread instead. But there was one part of him that starved until death, and that was his pride. Although he filled his life and mind with the word 'man', he doubted it and this doubt, working slow, taking its time in the years, the six of them, had bred bitterness inwardly. His cup was flowing over.

'I tell you anyman, *anyman* I tell you – I tell you go to hell Mister. Go to hell and cook for your black sins.'

But there was no man in his world to tell this to. Even when he threw back his head and shouted it up at them they were too far to hear. They only smiled and sometimes called him Little Father,

Little Baba, which was that word in his own language. Even the children, the youngest of them, those who had just discovered their legs, stood taller than Morris Tshabalala.

When he stopped again he had negotiated two blocks of Main Street and had reached the corner where a lanky, mournful-voiced individual sold newspapers. Although they had never spoken to each other, a nodding relationship had been established between them. The newspaper seller had been at that corner almost every evening for as many years as Morris Tshabalala had been crawling down the busy street to his supper at the Bantu Eating House. *Lay-ee-deeshin*, he called. A few minutes ago a van had off-loaded bundles of newspapers. *Cit-ee-deeshin, layeet-spotreesilts*. He was doing good business. Attracted like motherless souls to his cry, white people stepped out of the throng, bought their paper, and even as they scrutinized the headlines, were carried away again by the crowds shuffling past.

For a few happy minutes Morris Tshabalala believed his fears to be unfounded. His pursuer wasn't to be seen. He strained his eyes in the effort to see through the milling, aimless mob, but he was gone, either lost or grown tired and turned back.

'*Layeedeeshin,*' the lanky one lamented high over his head. In his own language and an even sadder tone he spoke to the cripple. 'They've shot a hole in the moon, strue's gawd. I have read. A hole in the ole moon. *Lay-ee-dee-shin –*' He sold a few more papers. 'What is going to shine at night?' he asked the world in general.

During a pause in the business of selling, he dropped to his knees and cut the strings around a bundle of newspapers.

'What else do they say?' Morris asked him.

'Irish Fancy by a length, at seven to two. She lead all the way.' He stood up. '*Lay-ee-deeshin. Spotreesilts.*'

They kept on buying. There seemed no end to the people who wanted to know about the moon and Irish Fancy at seven to two. Morris Tshabalala looked at them without charity. His awareness of the man following him had been a dead drag to his already tired body. But finding him gone had lightened his heart only momentarily. His freedom from anxiety became a freedom to realize with greater clarity than ever before the extent of his infirmity and the gulf that separated him from the rest of the unworried world. Had he been a man he would have taken sticks and beaten the little bastard to death. Instead he had to crawl away like a frightened dog with his tail between his legs. He looked at the street and the big cars with their white passengers warm inside like wonderful presents in bright boxes, and the carefree crowds of the pavement, seeing them all with baleful feelings.

It is for your gold that I had to dig. That is what destroyed me. You are walking on stolen legs. All of you.

Even in this there was no satisfaction. As if knowing his thoughts, they stretched their thin, unsightly lips into bigger smiles while the crude sounds of their language and laughter seemed even louder. A few of them, after buying a newspaper, dropped pennies in front of him. He looked the other way when he pocketed them.

He saw the man again quite by accident. Someone had dropped him a penny and he was pretending to be looking at something across the street while feeling around with his hand for the coin.

The man was standing in the doorway of a shop, and he was watching the cripple now with frank and open interest.

'You stool of a whore!' Morris murmured. 'You foul-smelling stool of a diseased whore.' Morris Tshabalala was a man, and now, only half the man he was, he is still enough for you. The night is long, and you will need patience, dog! He dropped down onto his hands and shuffled off.

The lanky, sad-voiced one called out after him: 'Your money, Little Father.'

Go to hell, Morris thought.

'Little Father, your penny!' He threw the coin in front of Morris who let it roll away into the gutter.

Here I am safe, he was thinking. Where there is light and people I am safe. This world keeps its lights and people until late. He can still lose patience or meet friends. A policeman might stop him and ask for his pass. Please God, let a policeman stop him and ask for his pass.

Now that he was on the other side Morris was able to watch him without having to stop. For the first time in six years the cripple did not notice the length of the street and the time it took him to reach the corner where he turned to the left. A lot of thoughts came to him, but many of them had no meaning. Are his hands soft? he would ask himself, and then shake his head in anger and desperation at the futility of the question. But no sooner did he stop asking it than another would occur. Has he got a mother? This question was persistent. Hasn't he got a mother? Didn't she love him? Didn't she sing him songs? He was really asking how do men come to be what they become. For all he knew others might have asked the same question about himself. There were times when he didn't feel human. He knew he didn't look it.

The small side street that would have brought him out near the eating house was an unanticipated and major problem. It was deserted and badly lit. Its very shortness was its danger because even when people turned into it, they were out again in a few seconds, and then it remained empty for a long time. Even if he were to follow someone in, he would be sure to be left alone. He knew from experience that even the slowest walker was too fast for him. On top of this was his hunger and thirst. Without realizing it he had been exerting himself and now his armpits were clammy and had soaked right through his old coat. Drops of sweat shone like jewellery on his wrists and throat. Tsotsi was still on the opposite side of the street, watching his victim through the gaps in the traffic rushing past. Morris knew that if he was caught in that street alone, it would be the end. There was a solution of course. To leave the money at the first lamp-post where it could be seen. He despised himself for this thought, almost as much as he despised himself a long time ago for taking the money.

His salvation was announced by a blare of impatient hooters and it came in the form of an old decrepit car that had stalled a little way down the busy street. It was streaked with dust, strapped high with baggage and crowded, mostly with women it seemed, because only two men got out to push. They got as far as the corner, much slower in this than Morris Tshabalala, and there after cursing and a lot of fist-shaking together with the laughing from the women who were hiding their heads they managed to turn it into the side street. The other cars, the ones with the loud hooters, ground their gears with impatience and roared away, shouting at the car that had stalled and getting it back in good measure. The two men took off their coats and looked down the street.

'Hell Piet!'

'Ja Stefanus.'

'That's a thing man.'

'Just like that hey.'

'Just like that man.'

'So what do we do?'

'Push man. It's not far.'

But first they sat down on the back bumper for a cigarette. The one called Stefanus banged on the back window. 'You laugh now,' he said, 'okay. But wait and see,' whereupon the women burst out laughing again. The men rolled up their sleeves, their cigarettes dangling between their lips.

'You know what I think it is?'

'No.'

'Distribiter.'

'Yes.'

'Impatient buggers hey. Strange place this Piet. Look at that poor kaffir there. Shame hey.'

'Ja Stefanus.'

'Okay man. Back to work.'

'Ja.'

And so they pushed, swearing again, panting before long, pausing once, and all of this to the renewed giggles of the women and in time to the slow rhythm of Morris Tshabalala who followed in their wake.

The sidestreet led into another wide thoroughfare which ran diagonally away from the main street. In its way it was just as big and busy, but not as bright. Walking down it you passed through a fringe world of unkempt, squarely ugly, mostly double-storied buildings whose doorways led off the pavement into darker corridors and cement grey backyards. At ground level there was a host of nondescript little businesses run by whites, Indians and an occasional coloured, all of them existing like small parasites on the lumbering, unconcerned body of Africa. In the rooms above them could be found everything from cast-off white men lying on their beds and staring vacantly at the ceiling to shyster lawyers and pass book racketeers. In the side streets were factories and warehouses. A few of the big hostels for bachelor Africans were also in the neighbourhood. During the day the workers were here in their thousands and at lunch hour they sat about on the pavements, talking sport or politics and playing draughts. When the whistles blew they went back to work until five o'clock when the whistles blew again and they went home, pouring out like ants hurrying about the chaos of a broken heap.

In the Bantu Eating House Morris banged on the front of the counter and called up his order. 'Dish of soup penny extra' – which meant you got a piece of meat floating in it – 'and six breads with butter.' The proprietor, Marcus da Souza, known to his customers as Susa, carried the soup and bread to a chair in a corner which Morris used as his table. Sometimes he teased the cripple.

'How is business? You make a lot today?'

'Bloody stinking lot of white people. Here is your money and go back.'

'You're rich, I know you. You're richer than me.'

'Go on back I tell you! Leave a man to eat in peace.'

Tonight Susa was tired, and Morris hardly noticed him when he paid for his food.

It was a cheerless room, and reflected the poverty of a people who measured their essentials and excesses in the smallest unit of the white man's money. Everything sold in the shop was a multiple of the humble penny. The bread went at twopence a slice, the pudding cake at three, coffee was fourpence a mug, the cold, oily hunks of fish sold at five, meatballs at six and the soup at seven. These prices had been painted on the door of the Bantu Eating House by Sam, the kitchen boy. He had left out the penny sign beside each numeral. He didn't think it necessary.

The room was furnished with long tables and flat wooden benches for seats. At one end was the counter. On it were two trays, the one holding the heavy, black slabs of pudding cake, the other piled high with slices of bread. Usually there were four trays but the fish and meatballs were sold out. The walls were a sombre, dark green and from the ceiling hung a few flypapers crusted over with the dry bodies of their victims. The only decorations in the room were a calendar advertising a lotion for straightening curly hair and a notice in grammatically bad Shangaan. It had been painted in black on a piece of cardboard by the same untutored hand of the menu. It read: 'This place knows no credit.'

Morris ate his food in silence. When it was finished he ordered another two slices of bread. When that was finished he crawled to the door and looked out into the street. He saw lots of people that looked like the tsotsi who had followed him, but not one that seemed to be purposefully waiting or watching the eating house. He went back to his corner and ordered a mug of coffee. It was nine o'clock and he felt safe. The Bantu Eating House closed at half-past-ten on Saturday nights.

Three other men were at a table, talking in low voices. From time to time someone would come in, take something to eat or drink, and then leave again.

Morris finally confessed to himself. You were frightened. He directed his thoughts at the rubbery reflection of his head in the mug of coffee. It was hot and he blew on it before taking small sips. You were frightened. His reflection nodded up and down in agreement.

You thought you had no fear. But tonight it was there, like a worm in your bowels. A small fear of death.

When the next thought came it was so great he put the mug down on the chair and rested his head against the wall, as if staring at the fly papers. He saw nothing. I want to live. I didn't know it. I wanted to be on the streets again tomorrow. I want to sit through another day on another corner. I want to be coming back here tomorrow night for supper. What's left of me still wants to live.

'Friend,' the voice was saying. 'You didn't hear me.'

'I was thinking,' Morris said.

'Not now. I mean at the corner.' It was the thin, sad-voiced man. He put a penny down on the chair beside Morris's coffee. He sat down at a table, but in such a way that he could still see the cripple.

'You left it behind. I called you but you didn't hear. I threw it but you let it roll away into the gutter.' He took a greedy mouthful of bread dipped in the soup. 'A penny buys a box of matches. One penny and you can set the world on fire.' Newspaper headlines had given him a bent for the bold, dramatic touch.

Morris picked up the coin and looked at it.

The newspaper seller watched him and when he had swallowed what was in his mouth he spoke again. 'People will kill for a penny,' and then as if replying to his own statement: 'There is nothing that somebody won't do.'

Morris put the penny away in a linen tobacco bag with his other money, and then told the man about the tsotsi who had followed him.

The thin one threw down the crust of his last slice of bread, lit a cigarette and listened in silence. He had large, sorrowful eyes. The sockets were wrinkled underneath as if by the weight of the eyeballs.

'They're dogs,' he said when Morris had finished, 'mad dogs. They bite their own people.'

'If I had my sticks,' Morris said, 'and I was a man, I would have killed him.'

The news vendor shook his head. 'It wouldn't help. Man dies in back street fight. One arrest. They'd hang you. It always happens. They always hang somebody.'

'So what does a man do?' Morris asked.

The thin one stubbed out his cigarette and stood up. 'Go home,' he said. 'Go home and pray to God on the way and thank God when you get there and don't see nothing. There was a story once. It wasn't my business. Man denies responsibility. That's us.' He said goodnight and left.

Morris finished what was left of his coffee, then went to the door. The street was almost empty. He could see no sign of the tsotsi.

Da Souza came behind him and looked over his head. He yawned and stretched. 'Tomorrow,' he grumbled. 'Tomorrow and yesterday. Hell!' He blew his nose in a handkerchief. 'It's finished. Today is finished. I'm closing.'

With a sharp twist of fear Morris heard the door slam behind him and the bolts rattle home. He had been safe inside. Now he was in the street again. Still he could see no sign of the man, and like the thin one said you had to go home. There was nothing else to do, so he moved off. For some months now 'home' had been a derelict signalman's hut beside the railway line that some years ago had been used to carry goods to and from the factories in this area. It was no longer in use and would be torn up one fine day. Morris realized this but wasn't overworried. His first months in the city had taught him that there was a never-ending collection of places to sleep. He'd already had half a dozen homes.

To reach his present home he had to slip down another side street, and then along the loading bays of a factory. It was poorly lit, the lights were spaced at long intervals, and it was here that he realized that Tsotsi was behind him again. He heard the footsteps and looking back saw him silhouetted in the light of one of the lamps.

To reach the next light Morris Tshabalala had to crawl through a stretch of darkness. It seemed endless. He looked back repeatedly, expecting to hear the whisper of quick feet any minute. It took so long and took so much of him, not counting the blood from the cracks on his hands, that when he reached the light he smothered his tears and paused for breath, and then finding the brightest spot he took out his money and held it high for the other one to see before putting it down. It lay like a small but lustrous silver spot in the dust.

At the light after that he looked back to see what would happen, and what he saw was more terrifying than anything he had expected. The young man walked up to the heap of coins, looked down at them for a few seconds and then kicked them flying into the darkness. And came on after the cripple, who then started throwing stones. There were plenty lying around and some of them were as big as a man's fist. Morris Tshabalala had had powerful arms as a full man. Six years of dragging himself through the street had doubled that strength. He threw hard, and with accuracy, stealing a few feet between every throw. It was a good idea because if he had hit the young man once, it would have been the end of him. As it was, all he succeeded in doing was to make him jump once or twice, and duck when they came hurling towards his head, rebounding harmlessly further down and skipping off into the darkness.

Crawling forward after one such throw, Morris Tshabalala looked back and could see no him no more. He knew then that the young man was keeping to the shadows and darkness and that the moment was near.

If I can't see him, he can hear me – and it was with that thought that he started swearing. He filled the night with obscenities, roaring them between his tears, throwing the words with even more violence than the stones. He kept it up until his voice cracked and was only a whisper. A few minutes later, a few more feet and he was in the final darkness beyond the last light and he knew that he had come to the moment and the place for which the young one had waited so patiently the whole night.

$$=7=$$

Tsotsi afterwards realized one thing about that night. His mistake was that he let the cripple reach Main Street. He should have taken him after he left Terminal Place. There had been enough time and chances. What is more, he would have had the advantage of complete surprise because the cripple hadn't realized he was being followed until almost at the end of the deserted street. But instead, and for a reason he could only guess at in terms of what happened later in the night, Tsotsi let him escape into the safety of the bright lights and big crowds. Allowing that to happen was in its way like the bluegum trees. It led to a lot.

Their actual meeting came as a moment of sudden terror. It was purely by accident that Tsotsi stepped on the hand. It was an even purer coincidence that just before it happened he had started thinking yet again about the baby, the bluegums, and the bitch. So compelling and exclusive was the power of his mystery that momentarily he had forgotten about Butcher and Die Aap, and where he was and why he was there. By agreement the three of them had wandered off separately into the crowds with their eyes and ears open. Tsotsi was asking himself again why it was that the bitch crawled so far and no further, always almost reaching him, but not quite, and what was the meaning of the dumb fear inside himself when he saw her. Coming at that moment the oath 'Whelp of a yellow bitch!' had torn into his thoughts, stampeding them into a split second of chaos and terror. When, almost simultaneously with his oath, Morris Tshabalala had pushed away the offending foot, it had felt to Tsotsi as if the bitch had at last reached him and was at his legs with her yellow teeth.

The moment passed in a blink. When he looked down at the pavement his thoughts fled and his terror lingered in his heart only as the troubled echo of its passing. His mind would have been a blank were it not for the burning hate of the cripple at his feet. It turned so violently in his guts that he almost kicked him. He remembered in time that he was in Terminal Place and that the crowds were big enough to be brave with a man who kicked a beggar. But he remembered also the hour and his purpose. What happened next was as natural in the pattern of his life as waking and sleeping were in those of other men. I'll take you, you bastard, he thought. Tonight I'll take *you*. His choice was made.

In terms of hard economics, of the profit of the job measured against the likely loss of a life, the choice was indifferent. Those beggar boys never made that much that it was worth following one away when you could have just as easily piled your gang into a taxi and taken your chance at the driver somewhere along the road back to the township. They were much more the game of those younger years when you had got tired of snatching in shops and were beginning to think of bolder and bigger schemes. But it was typical of Tsotsi to act at times in disregard of the hard and fast rules by which those like himself had learnt to live. It was this perverse streak in his nature that made him pick one specially for Boston the previous evening, and had now chosen one for himself.

It was his ugliness, the slow, creeping deformity of the man that kept Tsotsi faithfully behind his back. He studied him with fascination. In the crowds of Terminal Place he was able to follow unobserved and yet get close enough to hear the swinish grunt the cripple made after every reach of his long arms. He caught snatches of the lunatic conversation he kept up with himself. Once he was so near that looking down he saw where three deep creases had already been groined into the neck by the repeated effort of forcing the head back so as to see ahead. The beggar had to do just this from time to time and Tsotsi noticed that the skin folded up and bulged out like the ropes of a double-stranded noose, and then he looked like a dog who had been pulled up short by a savage jerk of its leash. His hands were the same lifeless grey of the pavements. Their nails were almost bluish-black.

When the man crawled out of Terminal Place, Tsotsi was forced to drop back in case he became suspicious. This did nothing to dampen his morbid interest. If anything it increased it, because from the perspective of a few yards he noticed details that he had missed before. At that distance he could see the first budding of the hump he would one day carry like a mountain on his back, if he lived long enough. There was also the thing about his movement. It was all in the arms. From the shoulders down he might just as well have been a sack of potatoes because he dragged himself like that. In this he reminded Tsotsi of something. At first he couldn't think what it was, and when he did remember he was excited. He moved like the bitch of his memory. It was a comparison that worked both ways because it also revealed something about the bitch that he had not realized. Her back legs had been useless, too. She had used only the front ones, like him.

After this discovery Tsotsi's interest in his victim rose to an obsessive intensity, and he let his time and opportunities slip by. This man, this half-man, this unsightly and disfigured remnant of a man Tsotsi recognized with all the certainty of his unnumbered years as being the true figuration of life. He was a symbol of this precisely because he was bent, and broken, and so without meaning that other men had abandoned him. This was the final reality to life. Everything else was just rouge and lipstick on an ugly face. Smiles and laughter changed nothing, no more than a new pair of trousers would have given the cripple his legs.

Tsotsi was convinced of this. The conviction was so absolute it was part of himself, of his life and of his way of living. It was there like the blood in his veins and his heartbeat. Where it had come from he did not know, but he had it. He had a deeply intimate and personal knowledge of the grotesque anatomy of life.

He had never seen it so clearly, though. In the past it had come like a bad aftertaste to those moments when unavoidably he had been brought to the brink of a memory. It had been like that after the incident with the policeman and his prisoner, the one who had recognized Tsotsi and called him David. For days afterwards Tsotsi had brooded and it wasn't upon the man who had cried: 'It's me, Petah.' He had known it was better to forget him, and had promptly done so.

Tsotsi brooded because when he had finished that dice game with Butcher and Die Aap, and the man's hopeless cries were heard no more, he had stood up and seen the truth again so clearly he wondered why it was that he kept on forgetting it. The world was an ugly place. It was the ugliness of things that had gone crooked and were now twisted out of all meaning. It was a deformity that began with houses that had been badly matched to the bodies they held, being too small, or too windy or cracked open to the rain like the careless laying of an egg on sharp rocks. Then there were the bodies themselves. In the cruel confinements of their lives they had grown awry. The very effort of living was a pain. You could hear it in your bed at night if your ears had been sharpened enough by disgust. The world was one long wheeze and rattle as it laboured uncertainly in sleep. Butcher's hands were another living embodiment of this reality. So too the dead face of Gumboot Dhlamini, the one they had taken on the trains. It was true of all life. The only trees in the township, those around the cemetery, had expressed it in their stunted growth, drawing out the full meaning in their misshapen silhouettes seen against the windy sky. It amounted to the basic horror of existence.

There were days, of course, long, unconscious stretches of time when he didn't realize it, or had forgotten it in the way men lose their deepest convictions in the morass of their daily lives. Then, when something else happened that nearly got him remembering, like the time he watched the spider spin its web, or when he smelt damp newspapers, it was back again and his eyes, as if given the miracle of real sight, saw the truth.

But never had the experience been so intense, so focused as that twilight time when he walked out of Terminal Place. Ahead of him crawled the truth as he had never seen it before, rolled up, convoluted, twisted into itself in one human parcel called Morris Tshabalala.

It was not long before Tsotsi realized that he had made a big mistake in letting the cripple reach the Main Street. He'd known all along of course that once it happened he would have to wait for another dark and deserted spot before he could take his money. But he thought it would only be a question of following his man and being ready when the right moment came.

Then he discovered that something else had got involved. It happened when Morris Tshabalala rested at the corner where the man was selling newspapers. Tsotsi saw him look back, straining for a sight of his pursuer, and something of his relief when he thought he had shaken him off. With even greater clarity he saw his fear a few minutes later when he spotted Tsotsi on the opposite side of the street. This was the moment, and what happened was a feeling. It was totally unlike the hate he had felt when he first saw him in Terminal Place. It was also not the disgust that had welled up so strongly when he followed him. It was a feeling he seemed to know, and yet could not say he had felt before, and it had come when he saw the other man's fear. It came again when Morris Tshabalala dropped down and dragged off. It came yet again when he saw how much faster the cripple was trying to move, as if what lay ahead was better than what he had left behind. It occurred more frequently as time passed, so that a few blocks down the feeling was coming measured as his heartbeat.

Tsotsi knew that something was happening to him. But when he discovered the real nature of the feeling it had gone so far it was too late to do anything about it.

They had stopped again. It was obvious why. But maybe even if that dark little side street hadn't been there he would still have stopped, because he needed the rest. He looked even more like a dog when he was out of breath. His body had the same rhythmic up and down movement as when it panted. At that distance – Tsotsi was still on the opposite side – the light sometimes played tricks on his eyes and he imagined he saw a long tongue lolling out of the bent head. When he looked up, either to see down the side street or at Tsotsi across the road, or back over his shoulder, you thought he was going to howl, the way dogs did in the townships, sitting on their haunches in the empty streets when the moon was bright. One short and dark sidestreet, and the cripple too frightened to crawl into it. He was right of course, Tsotsi knew that. If the cripple moved down it, the time would have come to act.

While he watched the cripple and waited, Tsotsi kept saying to himself: I don't know you, fucker, not from nowhere, so what do I care. Just you make a move. I don't care a damn thing for you. It had never been necessary to say this to himself before. He had to now, and it was because of the feeling. Tsotsi had a growing presentiment of its nature, but it was not yet fully revealed. At that moment he still knew it only by its hidden working in his body. It was there as a lethargy in his legs that should have been stiff and ready to run when the moment came, as a tiredness in his fingers that would have to be even quicker if he was forced to use his knife. Above all else it was there as a desire – and even that in its way was dull and only half-formed – that it would be better if the cripple didn't move, if neither of them moved at all, and all of the time to come rushed past like the motorcars, leaving him against the wall and the cripple on his corner.

The full truth of what had happened to him came when the old car stalled and was pushed to the corner and he saw his man escape in its wake. He did care. Regardless of what he had been saying to himself a few minutes ago, he did care. There was no possibility of doubt or of arguing it away. When Morris Tshabalala crawled off behind the car, Tsotsi experienced a spasm of relief. He couldn't believe it of himself. He shook his head the way donkeys do to dislodge a troublesome swarm of flies. He cleared his throat and spat onto the pavement as if there were a galling taste in his mouth. He even closed his eyes and dropped his head back against the wall as if he had decided to sleep and forget the episode. The truth persisted. His man had escaped into a few more hours of troubled living and he was desperately glad. It was obvious now what had been happening to him as he followed Morris Tshabalala down the main street. He was also right in thinking it had never happened before. He had felt for his victim.

Tsotsi kept well back after that, and from the darkness of a doorway he watched the cripple enter the Bantu Eating House. There was an Indian shop opposite it, and beside the shop a soap-smelling alleyway with three dustbins at the entrance. They were so crammed with garbage the lids didn't fit. Tsotsi bought a few slices of polony from the shop, then sat down on one of the dustbins to wait some more, but above all to examine the strange experience of feeling for a man.

He refined the thought. The truth of the matter was not his feelings, but the other man's. It was Morris Tshabalala's fear, his desperation, the agony of his futile effort to escape, his gladness when the inevitable had been deferred for a little while longer.

But how had it happened that he, Tsotsi, who had done so much more to so many others, had had to wait until that night before realizing something of what the other man felt? He could only guess at the answers. Groping blindly, his thoughts at times brushed the truth as when suddenly, and irrationally it seemed, he remembered

Boston being sick after the job on the trains. He felt there was a connection between this new experience of his and that moment of Boston's. But the full meaning and miracle of sharing in another man's suffering eluded his stumbling attempts to catch it. In retrospect there was only the long, painful and silent pursuit down Main Street and how somewhere in the course of it the ceaseless magnification and focus of his interest in the cripple had found a crack and a way into the experience of his flesh. That is what it was. The experience of Morris Tshabalala's flesh.

What is sympathy? If you had asked Tsotsi this, telling him that it was his new experience, he would have answered: like light, meaning that it revealed. Pressed further, he might have thought of darkness and lighting a candle, and holding it up to find Morris Tshabalala within the halo of its radiance. He was *seeing* him for the first time, in a way that he hadn't seen him before or with a second sort of sight, or maybe just more clearly. The subtleties did not matter. What was important was that in the light of his sympathy the cripple was revealed.

But that wasn't all. The same light fell on the baby, and somehow on Boston too, and wasn't that the last face of Gumboot Dhlamini there, almost where the light ended and things weren't so clear anymore. And beyond that still, what? A sense of space, of an infinity stretching away so vast that the whole world, the crooked trees, the township streets, the crowded, wheezing rooms, might have been waiting there for a brighter, intense revelation.

After only one bite the polony fell unnoticed from his hands. Feeling as if he had drunk too much, Tsotsi lurched to his feet and around to the front of the shop. He wanted to see himself. He was sure he looked different, that he would see on his person some sign of the past few hours. A new head maybe, with other eyes and strange lips speaking different words. There were none of the mirrors that some of the big shops had in Main Street. But a little way down he caught the ghost of his reflection in the display window of a shoestore. The light of the pavement was too dim for it to be clear. When he moved up to the glass his image disappeared. He could only see it standing well back, and at that distance and dimness he recognized nothing except the shape of a man. It could be me, he thought, or Boston, or Butcher, or even the beggar if he had legs. There was a comfort in this thought.

The door to the Bantu Eating House was being bolted and locked. A second later the lights went out. Almost in panic, Tsotsi looked around the street. I've lost him, he thought. He's got away. He ran very quickly back the way he had come. There was no sign of the cripple. At the side street where the cripple had escaped behind the car, Tsotsi stopped. Why have I come back – maybe he's gone forward. He was out of breath, but ran back even quicker to the Bantu Eating House and then beyond it. When he saw him, his relief escaped in a small, hysterical laugh.

My man. I nearly lost you. I have found you back. My poor, slow man. I'm sorry. I tell you I'm sorry my poor slow man. But what can I do?

There was nothing he could do, but drop back again into the shadows, and follow, waiting for the right moment. It was inevitable, like sunrise, or sunset. You chose a man, and you kept after him until it was over. His new found sympathy regretted this. It pained him to see the tired and slow way the beggar moved, thinking that he was at last safe. But what could Tsotsi do. He had chosen and this was his man. With each step, each drag nearer their appointed meeting, his sympathy cut deeper until the time came when it felt as if his feet and his heart were pointing in opposite directions and that no one way was forward for all of him. There was no conflict. It wasn't a question of should I or shouldn't I. That didn't exist. He was resigned to the inevitable, watching it unfold as doctors would the last stages of a disease in a patient who is beyond help.

Tsotsi waited with painful anticipation for the moment when Morris Tshabalala would realize again that he was being followed. It seemed it would never come. Either because he was tired or not caring or feeling completely safe, the cripple did not look back once. It reached a point where Tsotsi could no longer stand the strain. He made noises. He coughed, he whistled, and when Morris Tshabalala started crawling past the loading bays, Tsotsi came the closest he had been since Terminal Place.

At last it happened, and from that moment – the cripple looking back white-eyed at Tsotsi who paused under a lamp – the last minutes before their meeting exploded as violently as the preceding hours had been slow, slow in their torture and accumulation of terror.

First the money, piled by the cripple into a careful heap in the light. This was the justification – of everything. Of the choice on the crowded pavement of Terminal Place, of a terror that had broken a man's spirit more surely than his body had been halved by a falling beam in the chaos of a mineshaft, of useless sympathy burning now like a small candle where darkness would have been better, and Morris Tshabalala had put it down, the lustrous heap of it, as if, like a full stop in the middle of the night, it would end the rhythm of Tsotsi's feet and cancel what was yet to come. It was cheap. Death would have been a bargain at that price, and now it was trying to buy life. A sense of outrage at its belittlement of all that had happened gripped Tsotsi. He kicked it flying into the night, and it was not just for his own sake but for the other man's as well.

As if in retribution for this action, the stones came hurtling at him, making him skip and dance like a puppet strung from an epileptic hand. Tsotsi wanted to call out: I understand, my poor slow man, I understand. But he was forced into the darkness where the obscenities came flying at him with as much violence. They were broken only by the sobs, and even though they were not meant for him. They were the most terrible of all when his voice cracked.

Tsotsi had circled and was waiting in front, squatting on a cement platform, in the final darkness beyond the last lamp-post.

He waited until the cripple stopped a few feet away. Then he waited for silence, and after the sobbing and strangled breaths had quietened, he waited to be seen.

Their meeting was wordless. They didn't need them. Into a few silent seconds they crowded the intimacy of a lifetime, so that when Tsotsi eventually did speak it was as if they had known each other for ever.

'What do you feel?'

'Nothing.' His voice was hoarse, the words rushing like wind through a leafless tree, dead from drought.

'Nothing?'

'It is over. Feeling is over.'

'What did you feel?'

'A fear of death.'

'No more?'

'No more.' Morris Tshabalala lent back against the ramp. It was the position of his poverty, of the long, empty hours on a street corner while he waited for pennies to fall. But with this difference. He looked up, resting his head against the wall, and not just because he was tired.

'No more. It is the lesson of my hands. I have this night learnt it in my heart.'

'Tell me,' Tsotsi asked.

'My hands held life.' Tsotsi waited. 'My hands felt it. Ow! I picked nipples like berries and the women cried with happiness when they moved to the secret parts. Then came ...' He searched forward.

'Speak man,' Tsotsi asked when the pause had yawned out into seconds, and then minutes.

'The sky fell down. The world turned upside down for me and I walked through life on my hands. You have seen. You have seen enough. These hands no longer feel. Now my heart no longer feels. Tonight my manhood fell down and crawled beside me and felt fear, and felt it so much it no longer feels it. You have seen. You have heard a big man cry. It is enough.'

'It was the worst of all,' Tsotsi said. 'Of all the things since we began, the crying was the worst.'

'What else was there?'

'You grunt. When you crawl you grunt like a dog thing.'

'What else?'

'You look like a dog man and I feel with you, but now I want to know. How do you piss?'

'Sitting up, between my stumps.'

'Shit?'

'Bending forward as if I am going to crawl.'

'Woman?'

'Never. They laugh.'

'What do you know man? What do you know this night?'

'You took a long time. You are patient.'

'I tell you I felt for you man.'

'If I had my legs and my sticks I would have killed you. In a short time. I would have cracked your head open like a nut.'

'Bantu-boy hey. Me. I use a knife.'

'Now me. What have I done to you? I gave you my money. All my money from one day. I have nothing else.'

'I don't want the money, I kicked it.'

'I saw.'

'I tell you man I did feel.'

'Then why did you choose me, tsotsi?'

'You are ugly, beggar. You are the ugliest thing I ever did see.'

Morris Tshabalala heard this without anger. It was the truth. There had been more bitter things in his life.

'Is that all?'

Morris Tshabalala thought about the question unhurriedly. Was it all? No, there was still something else. And in its way it was the greatest of all. It was *his* revelation. But how do you touch a thing like that, or pick it up in words so that you can say it and hear it? There was a simple statement of it, but he hesitated, uncertain that four common words could mean so much.

'I want to live,' he said at last.

Tsotsi thought he understood.

'I want to live,' Morris Tshabalala repeated. 'You know that?'

'Yes,' Tsotsi said.

'No. You don't,' the cripple said, and for the first time in their talk his voice rang with an emotion. How could he know it? How could anyone know the full meaning from only four words. There was something like a lifetime clamouring behind those words. What else were the years he had spent crawling along the unending miles of the city pavements? Hadn't it begun with a moment as terrifying as that other birth from a woman's belly? Hadn't they dragged him out of an even darker womb to begin a sequence of days so different, so unlike anything he had ever known before, that it could only be likened to being born again? Time was relative. Measured by something other than days and months, his six years had made him an old man.

'No, you don't,' he said to Tsotsi, his voice quick and agitated at the rejection of so much of him. 'It is not just you and your knife. I say it to myself. Not to you. To my hard hands and my ugly face and my no legs. I say it after many years of thinking I was dead and tomorrow was nothing except maybe the day when the rest of me would be buried with the other pieces.' Morris Tshabalala saw it very clearly now; he was seeing it passionately, the truth, after all the years of thinking nothing mattered.

'What is it, what do you mean?' Tsotsi could see the other man's excitement. The cripple was sitting forward now, holding out both his hands as if to feel rain or receive a tremendous gift. But they were trembling, and the sight of them excited Tsotsi. 'What do you mean man. I don't know a damned thing what you're saying.'

'Sunshine,' he said. 'Sunshine in stones. The warm stones of the streets. I felt it tonight at the end of the day. I must feel it tomorrow. If my hands don't feel I'll make a hole in my trousers and sit with my soft bum to feel, or lay my face on the ground. There is also ...'

'What is there also?' Tsotsi asked. He was also trembling now with excitement. He didn't understand the outward meaning of the words. He didn't need to. Their intimacy at that moment was of so fine a nature that the excitement, the wonder of the cripple broke through the personal context of his words and touched Tsotsi.

'Rain. Falling down. And wind blowing, and trees growing, and the colour of things, and the streets where I have heard birds sing. Do you understand now? I want to live. Do you understand?'

'Yes man. I'm telling you all the time I'm feeling with you.'

'Why do you have to kill me, tsotsi?'

Tsotsi took an eternity to reply, or so it seemed to the man beneath him. And even when he did speak, the pauses between the words were so long it seemed men could be born and live and die in them.

'I don't have to.' This meant nothing to Morris Tshabalala until the young man said it again. 'I don't have to.'

Then Tsotsi stood up, and with something like a laugh he walked a little distance away where he stood for a long time with his hands on his hips.

Tsotsi did not go back to his perch on the wall, but like the other man sat down with his back to it a distance away in the darkness. He said it for the third time: 'I don't have to. It is over, beggar. I let you live.'

'How old are you, tsotsi?' Morris Tshabalala asked.

'I don't know,' he replied truthfully. 'But I will find out.'

Morris Tshabalala tried hard to see him, but because of the darkness there was only the shape of a man. He tried to remember what he had seen of him in the streets where there had been light, but all he could picture was his own terror. I must give him something, he thought. I must give this strange and terrible night something back for all it has given me. With the instinct of his kind, he turned to beauty and gave back the most beautiful thing he knew.

'Mothers love their children. I know. I remember. They sing us songs when we are small. I'm telling you, tsotsi. Mothers love their children.'

After this there was silence for the words to register and make their meaning, for Tsotsi to stand up and say in reply: 'They don't. I'm telling you, I know they don't,' and then he walked away.

He looked back. The cripple had crawled away to the lamp-post where the money was scattered and he was picking up what he could find.

The city is dead. With the life of its pavements drained away, the straight unpliant lines of the city lie exposed. Street lamps stick up like golden-headed pins holding it to the earth. They are the only light because now the shop windows are dark. At the taxi ranks the night drivers are slumped over their wheels in sleep. Tsotsi passes them because they only take whites. He also passes night watchmen, sitting on boxes in the doorways, wrapped up in old army coats and armed with knobbed kieries like brooding angels who have executed judgment. Soon Tsotsi is completely alone and then he moves like the last, small impulse in a dead body.

It was a long walk back to the township, but Tsotsi stopped only once on the way. Even then he had to try several times before finally succeeding. Because he wanted to stop. He needed to think. But each time he sat down – once on the closed-in seat of a white bus-stop, a mile later beside the fence of a lumber yard, and then after that just on the pavement of a dark street – each time he lost control of his thinking. Like a driverless car down a steep hill, his mind moved with gathering momentum past images and incidents until they were racing past so fast he didn't have time to recognize their meaning. They came without any sensible sequence. A shoebox, Boston drawing a thin line of blood across his arm with the knife, the mummified face of the baby blooming out into a black hole as it cried, then the bitch, then the beggar pissing between his stumps, then an Indian shopkeeper saying 'Very good baby milk ...' The inward acceleration of his thinking was terrifying. He seemed incapable of holding on to one thought long enough to avert the next one.

Walking helped because it stopped him thinking. He hung determinedly on to every physical sensation involved in picking up one foot and placing it in front of the other. He concentrated on the vague feeling he had of the pavement through the soles of his tackies. He studied the swinging rhythm of his arms and noticed that they were synchronized with that of his feet. But when he stopped again the same thing happened.

At first he would actually have to search for something to think about, as if his mind had stalled just over the top of the precipitous incline. What is there? he would ask himself. What is there to think about? This question was the push that brought him to the edge. 'The baby!' he would say and then he was on his way down.

The baby. Now, okay ... and Boston. Yes. Okay now ... and the bitch too, bluegums, shoebox, beggar ... and by then it was happening again and he would jump to his feet with a pounding heart and walk away.

Once he had turned his back on the centre of the city his way lay through an extensive factory area, where Tsotsi made his third unsuccessful attempt to stop and think. It was a world which must have had as its model the plaything precision of a child's blocks. The streets, crosslaid in the faultless squaring of a grill, were completely untenanted. Only once did he see a sign of life, when a car appeared at an intersection ahead of him. It nosed its way uncertainly across the street as if it had wandered in by accident and got lost.

At each corner Tsotsi passed he looked briefly, if at all, down another bank of vacant walls. The black squares of double doors, side entrances, high barred windows, chequered the night with another variant of the severe pattern. The street lamps, spaced at unvarying intervals along the edges of the pavements, added a final, strict rhythm to the monotony of the night with the movement of his shadow. Beside him, then ahead, then behind, passing in a strange, unageing metamorphosis from almost jet black to a greying insubstantiality that finally seeped away into the bricks, only to reappear later behind him and repeat the cycle. If Tsotsi had had eyes for such things he would have seen in the world around him an enormous model of the inward maze of his images, a world seemingly without beginning or end. It was not just by chance that he finally achieved his purpose and found his moment to think in something like peace only when he emerged out of his labyrinth.

More than anything else, the effect of turning that last corner was a sensation of space, of tremendous lift and room to breathe again as if a silent detonation that moment had blasted apart the ingrown complexities in the city. The road he had turned into was broad, and on one side dropped steeply into an expanse of uncrowded earth that cut deeply through the city like the dry course of a mighty summer-thunder torrent. This was the principal railway artery of the city and at the point where Tsotsi stood it had begun its gradual life out of earth before fanning out its innumerable pairs of parallel tracks to every corner of the country.

The city was strung out on the opposite side in a toothed silhouette that at the most stole a few paltry inches from the generous curve of sky overhead. A three-quarter moon had risen clear of the ragged building line and was shining with intense purity. It was at the moon that Tsotsi looked for the few minutes he paused on the corner. With his first sight of it, and the surprise of seeing it so unexpectedly, had come one thought. Its effect was a serenity as calm and cold as the moonlight itself.

It was the same moon of last night. Last night! The bluegum trees were last night.

A little way further the road skirted extensive marshalling yards. Tsotsi hurried down, eager to sit there and think. Beyond a heavy, metal fence was a stretch of weedy grass. He would be safe there from prowling police cars. It was a scene of melancholic and intermittent activity, as if the remnants of a herd of primeval, armour-plated beasts were kraaled here and their brute force trained into man's service. They filled the night with the shunt and snort of their labour. The ceaseless coupling and uncoupling of coaches, the jolting, jarring moments when engines hooked up, rang out in hard, metallic noise. A few of the big locos, black and steaming with sweat it seemed, stood massively still under the tall floodlamps. They whistled from time to time, mostly in a flat, whispery note like the penny flutes of the township streets. But just occasionally a whistle would stream out that was all sound, a clean, ululating endless vowel. Among them, moving like nonchalant shepherds, strolled lonely men with lanterns swinging in their hands.

Tsotsi took in the picture with one sweeping gaze. But it was at the moon that he again looked longest.

Twenty-four hours! Only one day had passed since his rest in the grove of bluegum trees. It was a thought that reduced to a tangible dimension the unexpected turning in his life. It made it possible for him to put everything in its place. He could start at the beginning and work his way through the strange sequence of events that were strung out like unmatched beads between his two midnight meetings, first with the woman and then the beggar. Looking back, it felt as if he had woken up to a day of another man's life. There had been no precedents in his days for feeding a baby or sparing a man's life. But now the experience of it had become his, an indelible part of his being, as he sat there on the bank of stubbled grass, under the moon, with engines grunting at his feet. It was his baby now, by the law of finders-keepers, hidden away in a ruin; it had certainly been his half-memory of the bitch, his full sympathy for the beggar.

So what now? Was it the end – had it been nothing more than a freak out-of-season storm in the dry climate of his life? Did he go back to his old pattern tomorrow and forget today, and wait in his room for Butcher and Die Aap and maybe Boston – yes, Boston, what the hell about Boston! – and together with them plan another job?

Tsotsi knew that moment that there was no turning back on that day and what had happened. He had a presentiment that it was only the beginning of something and that a lot more was to come. It wasn't that he knew, or thought he knew, what would happen next. But that one day had left him with an awareness of the strange and sudden turnings that life could take. There might be more ahead. There was still the baby, and tomorrow it would be clamouring for his attention. (He would feed it when he got back to the township and it was light.) There was still the bitch. More than ever before he wanted to find other pieces that went with that fragment of a memory. There was still his sympathy and the awesome discovery, the moment when the cripple had asked, 'Why do you have to kill me?', that it was for him, Tsotsi, to choose between life and death. What he had thought of as inevitable turned out to be wholly dependent upon him and his choice. This, more than anything else, was a thought that seemed to reach down deep and touch the hidden meaning of the past twenty-four hours.

Tsotsi had always thought about life as a straight line, as undeviating as the one he had taken earlier in the evening following the beggar from Terminal Place, as inflexible as the railway tracks that swept past him, leaving no choice but to be carried where they went. And because Tsotsi had no memories, and had collected none, there wasn't even the metaphorical going backward in time to something already past. There had only been the present, that one continuous moment carrying him forward without questions or regrets on his part. Now, it seemed, he was wrong. One day had shaken the whole basis of his life.

There were alternatives in life. He'd had an inkling of this earlier in the afternoon with Butcher and Die Aap in his room and his inability to choose their job for that night. What he had since learned was that the alternatives were even greater than he had imagined. It was not just the sort of job, a choice of the ways and victims – killing itself was a choice.

A question shot with the impact of a bullet into his mind. When had he made that choice? Trembling with a confusion of anger and excitement he stood up and looked around desperately. When and how had he made the choice in the first place?

Then, as if he had stood up only to take the full weight of the past day on his shoulders, his knees buckled and he sank back to the ground. It was more than he could carry. The outburst of emotion ebbed away, and with it the last reserve of his strength. He curled up on the ground and slept.

An engine whistle blew out like a white ribbon in the wind.

=8=

The bell of the Church of Christ the Redeemer is tolling. It has a double stroke.

Ding-dong-ong-ong. Ding-dong-ong-ong.

In the pauses, the echo of the last note floats away from the belfry, low over the rooftops, circling the township like a heavy and grey bird. The shadow of its passing is Sunday.

Ding-dong-ong-ong. Ding-dong-ong-ong.

It is heard in the streets. Stepping staid and correct in the first response of their worship, a few move to the top of the hill where a few more are standing around the church door, waiting for organ sounds and the singing of the first hymn. The rest stay behind in the streets, sitting on steps or just standing, but all of them in the sun. They also hear and respond faithfully with the litany of their te deum.

'Sunday again.'

'Once a week and always on time.'

'Saturday and Sunday.'

'Half-brother days.'

'Me? Don't even think they're cousins.'

'They always come together, like a woman and a baby. Take one and you also get the other.'

Ding-dong-ong-ong. Ding-dong-ong-ong.

It is heard in the rooms. There are many still asleep, in beds, on sleeping mats, with blankets or without, coupled or alone. They stir and mumble, caught clumsily between dream and drab reality. The church bells belong to both. It is the late and lazy day. The sound settles in the room, and they nestle deep in its feathered melancholy and drift off to another sleep.

Somewhere Boston hears it. It is a soft sound so he listens, letting it wrap around the fragile splinter of his consciousness. He is looking at a small piece of naked skin with one eye. The other is closed. He notices that hairs grow out of tiny, pinhead depressions. He doesn't know where he is, what time it is or what is going to happen next. He doesn't recognize his own arm. He hears the bell and minutely studies the skin and the hair. Nothing else exists and he doesn't dare move for fear of pain or shame. A door slams somewhere and he hears footsteps. The feet are bare and are walking on wood. He hears his terror. It is a thin screaming note in his ears that magnifies the footfall and silences the bell. Don't come near me, he thinks hysterically, don't touch me or talk to me.

Ding-dong-ong-ong. Ding-dong-ong-ong.

Then they stop. The Reverend H. Ransome gets up from his knees. On his way to the door, he passes the window. He stops and looks out. He recognizes the deceit in this small action. It is the desire to see and not be seen. But what he sees is so innocent he dismisses his deceit as unimportant. Then he warns himself against excusing small failings.

They are shuffling into the church, scuffing their feet on the mat at the door before going in. The feeling is there before he knows it. He finds himself angry, impotently angry with their best-suited, unsmiling and stiff devotions. Go home, he wants to shout. Go home. It's no good. I didn't know his name. Instead he fumbles in his haste to open the door and cross to the church. He prays on the way: 'God help me.'

He saw it as he came through the doorway, stepping lightly among the fallen bricks. He saw it clearly as an uncertain line that was scrawled all the way down the yellow, peeling plaster, right down to the shoebox, then over it and into the corner beyond. Seeing it he stopped, and with the strange irrelevance of a panicky mind he remembered an idle moment one afternoon with the others in his room, when his hands had found a pencil that Boston had left on the table. He had toyed with it for a few seconds, leaving a scribble of lines on the table-top, playing with it like that until he had looked up and seen something in Boston's eyes that had made him angry and deliberately break the pencil. Even though what he saw now on the wall was as meaningless, he studied it so intently that when he spoke it was as if he had deciphered a strange script and was reading the message.

'Ants,' he murmured aloud. 'Jesus. Ants.'

It was the condensed milk, of course. The top of the tin was an unbroken, liquid brown mass of them that spilt onto his hands when he picked it up. So great was his horror of them that when he felt them swarming over his fingers he dropped the tin and rubbed his hand furiously on his trousers. They were now pouring in an unending stream out of the two holes he had punctured in the top, as if they had rested inside at the very heart of the sweetness. The spoon was just as bad. A crystal white crust of the milk had dried on it and the ants seethed over it in a drunken orgy of excitement.

Tsotsi turned to the shoebox last of all. He was almost too frightened to lift the lid. The baby lay quiet, in a sleep so close to death he believed it to be that until a bubble rose to its mouth and burst silently, leaving a thin smear of spit to trickle away down the side to the waiting ants. There weren't many. It couldn't have been long since they had found a way in. But they were there, ringing the opened mouth like the thin edge of another lip. The foul stench again came from the box.

With this first look came an overwhelming sense of despair. Tsotsi knew it was a crisis and that he had come either with minutes to spare or minutes too late. He fought down a sudden desire to throw the lot, baby, condensed milk and spoon, deep into the ruins and never come back again.

Instead he took a deep breath, held it in, and went to work. First he got rid of the ants on the face. The baby awoke once in the course of this and cried feebly, moving his head a little to one side. Tsotsi noticed that the eyes had lost their focus. They were weak and watery and stared with a terrible vacancy up at nothing. It took him a few minutes to kill all the ants, pinching them between his thumb and forefinger. Then he moved the box away from that corner to another where there was also shade but no ants. He went back to the wall to deal with the column on the plaster. With his flat hand, and starting at the bottom, he began to stop it, grinding and rubbing his hand each time to make sure there was not a single survivor. The top of the column was out of his reach, so he piled up a few bricks and standing on that dealt with it in the same fashion. His last reckoning with the ants was to shake and blow the tin and spoon clean of them and then to stomp violently around the corner where they swarmed on the earth in a minute panic. Finally, he shovelled sand over the spot with his feet.

He went back to the other corner and looked down at the baby. A few survivors had crawled out of the folds of his swaddling clothes onto his face. Tsotsi killed them, using the same technique of thumb and forefinger, before sitting down beside it with his back to the wall.

He felt better. Killing the ants had restored some of his confidence. But the urgency of the situation remained, even more so now that he was able to see the baby unobscured by his first feelings of panic and despair. Tsotsi had dealt too long in death not to feel its imminent presence in the shoebox. The baby needed a lot, and he needed it quickly. Food, he thought. It must have food. It must also be cleaned again and wrapped up in other clothes. But food. Food first.

The condensed milk was useless. After he had cleaned the tin and spoon of a few struggling ants, and blown into one of the holes to get out a spoonful, because it didn't come easily, it was to find as many ants drowned and bogged down in the milk as he had found on top of the tin. Tsotsi left the corner and standing on the remains of a wall hurled the tin and spoon with all his force deep into the ruins. He remembered the cripple. Last night, he thought. It is passed. This is today. Another strange day. He left the wall and broke the momentum of thoughts that threatened to carry him away from the present.

Milk! I must get milk for him. He went down on to his knees and bent close to the baby, as if it might whisper a few words of advice or encouragement. He studied the face intently. Those eyes! They made him feel he wasn't there. Tsotsi brushed his fingers past in front of them. They didn't blink. The baby's breathing came in shallow, fretful little sighs ending with a tick-tick-tick-tick from deep in its throat as if something there were counting off a few seconds for every breath. A few seconds of what? Tsotsi put out a finger and touched the small pink palm of one hand and the fingers closed on his like the tendrils of a lazy anemone. He felt the tiny, moist hold with a palpitating heart. He had a name for his experience of that moment. He was 'feeling for the baby'. He remembered the cripple again.

After a few seconds he pulled away his hand, stood up and wiped away the moustache of sweat droplets on his upper lip. What was he going to do? 'Milk.' He said the word aloud so as to rivet his attention to the problem. What was it to be? Another tin from the Indian trader? He almost accepted the thought because of the immediate avenue of action it offered him. But Tsotsi had lost faith in condensed milk, and in the ability of his clumsy hands to minister to the needs of the baby.

Tsotsi noticed absently that the long smudge on the wall where he had attacked the column of ants had been pencilled in lightly again. He repeated his first strategy, but this time using both hands, slapping so violently that his palms stung. It was while doing this that he remembered the thought Butcher had suggested the previous afternoon when he teased the woman. Tsotsi went back to the baby with only half the new column of ants disposed of. He sat beside the baby with this thought, for a long time, because it was a long thought and took its time in passing before he knew its beginning and its end. But when he did, it was also to know the end of his dilemma. He had a plan and as a final part of it he stood up and took the baby out of the box, abandoning that because the stinking yellow muck from the clothes between its legs had soaked through to the cardboard. It was useless now, the bottom having gone soft and soggy. Tsotsi wrapped up the baby in his coat and left the ruin.

At the bottom of the street, not far from Tsotsi's room – you could lean out of his window and see the spot – there where the road had managed to steal extra inches of land from the shacks and hovels that crowded the side in a warped frontage of corrugated iron, biscuit tins, packing-case wood, sacking and of anything else that could be nailed or tied together in the basic design of a few walls and a roof; there in this widening of the street, littered with stones because feet, thousands of them, to be numbered in generations of coming and going, had worked away the loose sand and tramped down the remainder hard and firm; there in the middle of all this, snaking out of the earth in a length of grey piping, and this firm on a three-foot beam of wood, buried deep on the day when the ground had been soft and easy on the spade, there, solitary, important, indispensable, hated at times, enjoyed at others, stood the communal tap. This part of the street was known as Waterworks Square, and the tap was the only one in that part of the township.

They came to it, starting early in the morning, and then all through the day, still there when the sun set and then after that returning intermittently through the night to chase away the dogs gathered to lick up the drip, yet all it gave was water. They came to it with buckets and basins and babies on their backs and in their bellies, they came to it old and young, some so young they never remembered, the oldest now so far gone in living that at their last the most they could do was shuffle with the queue and keep a place for an absent one, and all it gave was water. They came to it laughing, they came to it silent, or singing or sad, and to all it only gave water.

And because they had to wait so long for it – at noon the queue would stretch back past Tsotsi's room – because there stranger met stranger in a common purpose, a common thirst, and you could talk there waiting in the queue about nothing or everything and never meet again; because there you could see the face of the baby heard being born last night, or that of the man who prayed so long and loud, or the one who beat his wife, or the wife herself, blacker for bruises; because of all this, more than just waiting for water, a dull enforced drag of hours wasted in the sun while you shuffled nearer the tap. That stocky length of wood and gurgling pipe was rooted in their lives.

In the Church of Christ the Redeemer its water was sprinkled on the newborn in a double baptism because the children, especially as soon as they could walk and carry, were sent into its servitude. In the same church there had been a sermon on patience the Sunday after the mêlée amongst the women when the water was cut off.

In the deeper intimacy of the smoke-filled rooms, in the living breath of their language it had been raised to the pedestal of idiom. It was a language sharpened by wits so that 'talk at the tap' caught click and consonant of women idle at gossip as they moved in starts nearer the water; and sharpened by truth in 'sweet as the water' because there was the story of old Jenkins Malopopo who had stood his turn through a hot day, empty-handed, so that he could have his last drink from it, straight from the tap you see, and then die; and birth too, and this story lived in the words 'a baby is born between drops' because one had been, there beside it, in the sun, and the mother had stood up afterwards and waited because her paraffin tin was not yet full.

Among those who took their turn in the queue that Sunday afternoon was Miriam Ngidi. She was eighteen years old and carried her baby on her back. When she reached the queue she put down her paraffin tin and prepared herself with a sigh of resignation for the long wait that lay ahead until she reached the tap. It would take her half an hour.

That was one of the things you learnt in the township without ever actually being taught – how to measure the time of a queue by its length. It wasn't as simple as it sounded, a question of so many feet meant waiting so long. The number of buckets and paraffin tins came into the equation. Even the tap itself was a variable. It alternated between a strong, resounding burst of water that hammered on to the bottom of the paraffin tins with a roll like thunder, and a liquid, weak trickle that whispered when it hit the bottom of a bucket and after that flowed silently. There was something of a law to this alternation. It flowed weakest when it was needed most, in the early morning, then again at noon, and at supper time. So unconscious had been the learning of all this that Miriam Ngidi made her calculations without realizing it. About three o'clock, maybe thirty people, mostly with one bucket each. She reckoned on half an hour.

Her baby was awake. He hadn't cried once during the walk from the room, and for the past few minutes he hadn't even moved, not even to pick at the ends of the knotted doek on her head which was his favourite game, yet she knew he was awake. It's still the same, she thought. In my stomach, and now on my back. I still know when he is awake or sleeping, then without being able to see, and now without having to look. Even so, she did, turning her head so as to see over her shoulder. It was sucking a thumb and looking up innocently at the sky with eyes as deep and as cloudless. He was six months old. When he heard the cluck-cluck of his mother's voice, he jerked his hand out of his mouth and waved it as if a friend stood far away in the distance. In those eyes, quietly serious, so wide they seemed to reflect great horizons, in the gesture of the small hand that seemed to beckon them in, she saw a portent of great manhood. A bolt of pride surged through her. Her son! Hers, Miriam Ngidi's baby – the man they would call Simon.

She picked up her paraffin tin and hurried forward. The queue had moved a few precious feet. When she stopped again it was to look down at the ground. The baby was going to sleep. You quickly learned the signs. The weight of him on your back seemed to increase in a strange way, yet it was the same baby. The little body relaxed and the shape of him – you could feel it, the arms and legs when he was awake – seemed to melt and merge into that same mysterious obscurity of the months in your womb. He was asleep. he was happy. The thought of her baby drifted out of her mind and somewhere else she heard that small voice that was hers, and was never silent and always asked the same question. 'Simon, where are you? Simon my man, where are you? My man. Where are you?'

She saw the face so clearly. If she looked hard enough she could see it in anything, and so clearly he had only to open his mouth and speak. 'Simon, where are you? What happened? What? Where are you now?'

How was it that a man, a full-blooded, big-bodied man who had fathered a child in a woman, in love, could walk to work one day and never come back. She had searched. Eight months gone as she was at that time, she had walked the six miles to the factory, along the same road that he had set out on confidently every morning and returned from wearily in the evenings. It was the time of the bus boycott and all the people were walking and Simon was that sort of man that when the people walked, he walked ... and not come back. No sign of him, no word, no memory. 'He just didn't come, Miriam. There was a lot. It was winter, sister, and dark in the mornings. It was a long walk. You never saw who walked beside you.'

'Simon, where are you?'

'They will jump up in front of you, my child, if you fall asleep.' The words, gentle, spoken with that soft echo in which youth hears the voice of old age, made Miriam start out of her reverie. The queue had moved again. She picked up her paraffin tin, hurried forward and then looked back to see who had spoken. He was an old man, but the first grey hairs were just appearing now from a lifetime of staring deep into the fire in smoke-filled rooms.

Miriam dropped her eyes. Her gaze had been too bold.

The old man saw the respect and laughed. 'They do jump in front,' he said. 'One day I never moved at all they did it so cleverly. It is the young ones, the children.' He was carrying a jam tin with a piece of wire looped through two holes near the top. He saw her look at it.

'My tea,' he said. 'On Sunday I have afternoon tea.' Then thinking of the queue again, he laughed. 'Sometimes I have my afternoon tea for supper.'

He asked Miriam her name, her age, where she came from and how many children she had.

For a moment a few of the inevitable questions concerning a man called Simon, which she had asked every stranger she met, were on the tip of her tongue. But she didn't speak. Catching herself in this gesture of defeat, she looked up boldly at the old man.

'My husband,' she said.

He listened gravely, pretending not to notice the lump that was choking back her words. Before she could speak again he inclined his head forward, drawing her attention to another movement in the queue. They shuffled forward and after that she tried again.

'My husband went to work and didn't come back.'

The old man listened, looking first at the stones and then at the sky.

'With the others he walked to work but didn't come back.'

'There were many like that,' he said.

'Did you see him, by any chance?' she asked. 'His name was Simon, Simon Ngidi, and he lived at 913, Block C. A big man, father, such a big, big, man ...' Her voice trailed off. She saw the answer in his eyes.

When it came to her turn at the tap she turned around and asked him for his tin, and filled that first and then waited while the tap ran into hers. When it was full, another woman helped her get it onto her head. She walked with her eyes fixed straight ahead, moving her legs as if the water in the paraffin tin on her head ran through her body and into them. At the same time the sense of weight in her movement had a perfect proportion to it; she walked with incredible grace.

Miriam managed not to think on the way back to her room, so that when she reached it the pain had passed and in between putting the baby to sleep and the water on to boil – because she was now earning a living for herself and the child as a washgirl – she was able to think about what the old man had said without wanting to cry.

He was right of course. Many had gone like Simon, swallowed up by the earth, it seemed, on the dark mornings of the boycott and whisked away before word could be got home. What he hadn't said was that most of them had come back since, to tell the same stories of summary trial followed by a few weeks in jail. Simon was one of the significant few who hadn't returned.

'Simon, where are you?' It was always here, in her room, in their room, bare of so much but crowded with so much more, only here that she asked the second question: 'Are you dead?'

Outside it was easy to hope. He could be somewhere in the crowds, around a corner, down a street. There were so many people in the world that it was easy to think that one of them might be Simon coming home. But here in the room, with the memories of the real man, the big, living, Sunday-lazy man, here life was so painful a memory that death had been from the first a possibility and now with time a probability. But she carried on. You had to. Tomorrow is no respecter of today's tragedy and comes along and makes it the past, the thing that happened and is over and in a way done with, and gives you another day to get through.

So she had carried on, outwardly adjusting the pattern of her life as best she could, like taking in washing, doing odd cleaning jobs in the nearby white suburb. Inwardly she had fallen into something like a possessive sleep where the same dream is dreamt over and over again. She seldom smiled now, kept to herself and her baby, asked no favours and gave none, hoarding as it were the moments and things in her life.

The knock on the door as always quickened her with a moment of excitement until she reminded herself that Simon would never have knocked. She had wandered so far away from the day to day realities of her life in the room, in the township, that for a few moments after opening the door she saw him as just another young man. 'What do you want?' she asked.

He just shrugged his shoulders.

It was the next movement of his, looking back to make sure that no one was about, that brought her down to earth. Miriam tried to slam the door but he was quicker and got his foot against it. Before she had even thought of screaming he had his hand against her mouth and had forced her back inside and into a chair, kicking the door closed behind him.

Her panic passed quickly into a blind, overwhelming fear for her baby. Involuntarily she looked to the bed. He saw this.

'If you try to run away or scream I'll kill your child,' he said.

When she shook her head agitatedly, he released her. Miriam watched him. When he went to the bed where her child lay, every muscle in her body and in her throat tensed for a frenzied attack. But he did nothing to release it, only bending down for a long and good look at the baby. He turned back to her.

'Come,' he said, and moved to the door. The first time he had spoken almost impassively. Now, in that one word, there brooded a weight of something as sombre as thunder.

Miriam shook her head.

'Come!' His voice was loud and hard.

She didn't shake her head this time, but still she made no move.

'If you don't come, I'll kill your baby. It won't take long.'

She shrunk back at his last words. He knew why, but it was a complicated thought to contradict so he only said: 'It's not that.'

'What then?'

'Come!' he roared, and smashed a cup to the floor.

'Can I leave the child?'

'Yes.'

'Can I get somebody to take him?'

'It won't take long. You'll be back.'

He walked ahead; she followed at a few paces, and not once did he look back to see if she was there. Only when they reached the door to his room did he turn and point so that she went in first. Tsotsi closed the door behind them and Miriam pressed herself up against the wall so that he had to drag her by her wrist to the bed. She began to moan softly, but stopped when she saw the baby.

He let her have a good look before speaking.

'Feed it.'

She showed no understanding of his words and because he had no others he put out his hands and with one wrench tore open her blouse, exposing her breasts. There was no vest or brassiere. 'Feed it,' he said again.

She brought up her arms to cover herself and backed away from the bed, shaking her head. It was worse than what she had first thought he wanted. The thought of that greedy, decrepit, foul-smelling bundle in rags on the bed at her breast filled her with horror. It was a violation of her body that brought to a sharp pitch the possessive, miserly twist in her nature.

'He's too dirty!' Miriam cried.

'Then clean him,' Tsotsi said savagely. 'Clean him and feed him.'

When she still hesitated, he took out his knife and gave her one last chance.

'Now,' he said. 'Now. Or I go back for yours.'

Miriam fought down her disgust and went to work. She washed the baby in a basin of water, which he provided, and when that was finished wrapped him up as best she could in the rags which came out of Tsotsi's clothes box in the corner. Once the baby was washed and cleaned, her first revulsion for him was passed, but there still remained the feeding. There was no point in delaying it. Closing her eyes, and cradling the baby on her lap, she put her nipple into his mouth. Her breasts were dry when he started sucking, but she knew enough to wait patiently and let him continue.

With the first pull of his greedy mouth on the nipple a sudden

wave of erotic feeling passed through her body. With an impercep-
tible movement her thighs relaxed. If Tsotsi had meant what she
had first thought to be his intentions and had taken her at that moment, she wouldn't have fought him for long. The baby had had
that effect on her, and before long his alien, rapacious sucking
opened the deepest reservoirs of her milk. He drank deeply.

At the end of half an hour Miriam took him away from her
second breast with a feeling of tremendous physical fatigue. 'He
has had enough,' she said quietly.

Tsotsi had been at the window, looking into the street, all that
time. He watched her bounce the baby on her lap for a while,
rubbing his back, before wrapping him up and putting him down
on the bed.

He lay quietly. Very gently, she touched the raw patches around
his mouth with her fingertips and looked at Tsotsi inquiringly.

'Ants,' he said.

She didn't seem to understand, so he said it a second time, 'Ants
man, on the wall,' but she didn't understand or wouldn't believe
him, so he closed his eyes for a few seconds and said nothing more.

Miriam buttoned up her blouse and tucked it into her skirt. She
hesitated at the bed, as if uncertain whether to stand up or to stay
longer. Again at the door, only a few steps away from the freedom
of the street, she hesitated with her hand on the doorknob, looking
back at the bed.

'Where's his mother?' she asked.

Tsotsi shrugged his shoulders. He had lost all interest in her
now. Miriam stole a quick, searching look at him and then fiddled
unnecessarily with her blouse.

'A bitch,' she said, 'a bitch in a backyard would look after its
puppies better.'

The words had a strange effect on Tsotsi. He turned slowly away
from the window and looked at her with large, frightened eyes.
'No,' he whispered.

Miriam thought he said 'Go'. She opened the door, then closed
it behind her and walked home.

His Sunday night now, come in a warm cloud of smoke and
darkness in the streets and moths raging in soft storms around the
lamp; come under a velveted spread of smudged stars and a
promise of the moon in the east where a white radiance is already
leaping off the rooftops of houses that way; come at last after the

hazy end to a day that loitered its way lazily through sunshine and prepares now for sleep with the widest yawn and longest stretch of the week. And wherever the people are gathered together in drowsy knots, in rooms, around fires in backyards, on street corners or drinking in the shebeens, words are thrown out dispiritedly like a dice game without a stake. The prospect of sleep and the passing of time recur like lucky numbers, but no one gets excited because no one stands to win. They lack of other things as well, like the news of the world, the weather, or women, but somehow it always ends up humming the same theme.

'This baby wants bed.'

'Me too.'

'Same here.'

'Forty winks man and no dreams.'

'Today took its time all right.'

'Makes you tired, and tomorrow is another day.'

'Monday man.' ... early morning Monday, the blue day and back to back-bending work and the beginning of another week.

'I'm asleep man. I'm telling you I'm asleep as I'm sitting here.'

'Me too.'

'Same here.'

... But they sit on, moodily, and mumble some more about Monday and how the days come one after another and time passes and you get old.

'Ja! I'm telling you a man gets old these days before his time. Look at me. One good Saturday night and I'm finished.'

'Trouble is it comes at the end of a week. You're all worked out. Should be the first day, I say.'

It was as if the flame of everything that burned in the township – love and laughter, even hopes and fears – had been trimmed down until even the talk was no more than a smoulder of life, pulsing as soft as the coal in the braziers which they dug out to light their pipes. With time even that goes out and they curl up in their blankets. The moon rises and the dogs break out into a chorus of yelping and barking. In a sleep no longer than any other night, the world winds itself up again to go running through another week.

Tsotsi sat through it all, wide awake through all the time that had passed since the woman left, still wide awake now with sleep lapping like a black tide through the township streets. The baby had cried once and he'd carried it until it stopped, then put it back on the bed and gone to his seat in the corner. He had no desire for movement. He was frightened of anything that threatened to disturb the memory that had come to him from a long time away. So he kept quiet and sat in the dark and remembered it again from beginning to end. He remembered it again and again, pausing only in the deep silence between each reliving to wonder how he had ever forgotten.

— 9 —

Someone is humming. It is a deep, undulating note, pitched so low that it could be the murmur of men around a fire, except that occasionally a word breaks through the surface of sound and then it is heard to be a woman. The soft, unfaltering tones enfold the listening child in the warm security of the one thought: Mother.

Another voice, that of a much older woman, calls out: 'Someone is happy,' and the first one breaks off her song to say, 'Yes Mama.' The words are rising in ripples of laughter which pass effortlessly into the song again so that you could not say where the one ended and the other began. Emboldened by the admission, she sings louder, phrasing the actual words at moments when they touch her happiness: '... after time, a long time ... a lonely time ... a shadow on the road ... and the cattle lowing at sunset ...'

He is in a small room, sitting on the floor, dividing his attention between his mother's voice – feeling absolutely safe in the sound of her presence – and the dizzy droning of a big, grey fly swinging drunkenly into the window high above his head. It has been trying to get through all afternoon and now its stupidity seems enormous. Don't they learn, he wonders. Don't they know about glass and seeing things through it. It is quite obviously exhausted. Every few seconds it drops to the windowsill and rests there or crawls around in circles before rising and trying again. Closing his eyes he can actually catch small chips of sound each time it butts the glass. Suddenly it is mother he hears again and follows a wave of her song through to the next splash of words ... 'kine lowing at sunset'.

When he opens his eyes he has forgotten the fly and looks down at the cotton reels between his outstretched legs, but can't think of a game.

There is a smell of woodsmoke in the room and he knows without turning that behind him in the backyard a fire is burning in a paraffin tin with many holes in its side. He also knows that it is late afternoon, because the light from the window has moved across the floor and up the opposite wall where it is now a square of bright orange next to the door. There is nothing in this world of that moment that he hasn't touched with a thought or his own hands. Nothing is new; not the cotton reels, or the bed, or the old black shoes under the bed, or the boxes and things in the corners, or the smell of woodsmoke and his mother's voice. Everything is where and how it should be, and he is comforted.

'What time tomorrow, my child?' It is the old voice speaking.

The song stops. 'He says to be here all day Mama.'

'Just like a man. The *whole* day.'

'What is one more day, in so many years Mama.'

'So many years my child.'

'Yes Mama.'

'One more day.'

'I will wait it Mama.'

'After so many years.'

'He will come. It will be at an end.'

'All the years.'

'David!' It is his mother and he waits in silence. 'David!'

'Yes mother,' he answers.

'The salt, my baby. Bring me the salt.'

The salt is in a tin on a shelf behind the bed. If he stands on his toes he can touch the bottom of the shelf with his fingertips, so he knows he is getting bigger because there was a time when he couldn't touch the shelf, not even if he jumped. But the tin is still beyond him, and he must stand on the bed before he can reach it. While he is climbing up he hears the voices again.

'Does *he* know?' It is the old voice.

'Yes Mama.'

'What does he say.'

'He is a child Mama, he was too young to remember.'

'So many years.'

Now he has the salt, and is down from the bed with a jump, and with another jump he is at the door and there he sees his mother on her knees before the porridge pot, beside the fire, and because she is beautiful and young and gentle he rushes to her and she catches him up in her arms, laughing as she hugs him, smothering him happily in her smell and her warmth.

Then he turns and looks at the old woman, watching her in silence because she is the oldest thing in his world and he has great respect for her and also fear. She is small and crooked and what is left of her is held in voluminous clothes. Her face is like the tortoise he once found in the veld and brought home. He respects her because of the example of the big people of his world, like his mother, who speak softly to her. He fears her because once when she found him doing something that was wrong, she caught him with that thin, bony hand of hers which looks like a fowl's foot, and with the other one pinched his bum until the snot and tears came into his mouth. But there is more than just the respect he had learnt from others and his self-taught fear in his attitude to her. He knows that she watches him carefully and sometimes sees him more clearly than the big people – even his mother – who have a way of looking but not seeing. What is more important, she has never laughed at him. Not once. That then is how they face each other now, himself silent, wondering if she saw him do anything today, and the old one eyeing him with her bright, black beads.

'Does he look like him?' she asks her mother, who looks up from the porridge pot to smile at her son.

'Yes Mama. He is our child.'

The old woman spits out a gobbet of the snuff she puts in her lower lip and calls him. He looks down at his feet, and fidgets on them until his mother says, 'Go to her David,' so he goes.

The old woman lets him stand before her, but does not touch him. 'How old are you young one?' she asks.

He looks back at his mother who says, 'Tell her, David.'

So he says, 'Ten years.'

This seemed to make her angry because she tried to spit again but failed because there was nothing in her mouth, so she snorted, 'Ten years. You're still in your mother's belly.' He had nothing to say to this and his mother was also silent, but not the old one. 'Ten years – you haven't even been born to the troubles of this world.'

This time his mother spoke, but softly, and using the same voice as when she chided him for being naughty: 'It will come Mama. It will come.'

The old woman sank into a brooding silence, turning her head deliberately so that she no longer saw him.

A minute later, when she seemed to have forgotten her presence completely, he left her and walked once around the yard, coming to a stop a short but safe distance away from the yellow bitch who looked up from her corner, eyeing him with even colder deliberation than the old woman. A step nearer he knew would get her to her feet, her upper lip curled back from her teeth, and another step would bring her snarling at him, straining at the end of the chain which kept her tied to a fencepole. She used to play with him, running up to his feet and rolling over on her back with her legs curled in air so that he could scratch her belly with his toe.

Then, quietly and unexpectedly, a few weeks ago, she had changed, and no longer played and didn't seem to recognize him anymore. This was a great pity and a great surprise. But only to him, because his mother didn't appear to notice, and even when he drew her attention to it she only smiled and shook her head. The old woman too, because he was persistent in these things. Surely she would have something to say about the matter, but he was wrong there because all he got out of her was a 'Mind your own beesness', and a jet of tobacco juice which not by accident was put down on the ground very near his foot.

So now, the safe distance from the bitch, he took the step which brought her to her feet with a rattle of the chain, and then got ready to run after the next because that had now become a game. But he didn't take that second step this time because his mother stopped him.

'Leave her, David.'

'She doesn't play any more.'

'You'll have other playmates soon enough,' his mother said. 'Go now and get the mat because the food is nearly ready.'

So he went and fetched the mat, the grass one rolled up in the corner, and laid it out for them to sit on. After that his mother gave him a plate of food for the old woman, who received it with a pretence that she didn't see herself take it, because she had no food of her own, no people of her own, and if his mother didn't feed her she would surely have died.

Then to the evening meal; facing his mother, the porridge between them and the meat on a plate, and the red coals in the paraffin tin keeping out the chill of the evening because by then even the sky was grey, and looking up he could already see one star; eating in silence for a long time, caught in the slow rhythm of their hands dipping in the pot, each taking a turn after the other, the only sounds in that silence coming from the old woman sucking a bone and the yellow bitch at the end of a taut chain, whimpering until tossed a bone. When his mother had finished eating and had wiped her hands and picked a piece of meat from a tooth, she looked at him, her son, playing with a few crumbs of mealiepap on his plate, and told him again that his father was coming tomorrow.

He couldn't remember when she had first told this story. It was the story of a man, a big man, a gentle man, a laughing man who had had to leave them for such a long time, but would come back one day. That was the manner of the first times she told him. One day, he was always coming back one day; and she had told it that way for many years and in a voice that made one day sound a long time away. He had had this story at supper most nights of his life, and maybe for this reason had not noticed the changes, like the time when he realized that her saying one day did not sound such a long time away, and after that failing to catch the precise moment when her voice, quickened with hope, spoke of a definite day, because the one day was said no longer. Instead she gave a definite day and a date, this still meaning nothing to him, until lately she had been saying things like next month, next week, three days time – and that he could understand in a way. Now it was tomorrow and that he could understand most of all because it simply meant going to sleep beside his mother, and then opening his eyes and there it was – tomorrow.

This man, this big, gentle, laughing man – his father – was coming tomorrow.

And what did he see when she said this? The image had taken a long time to form, and parts of it were almost as old as himself, going back many years, to the time she said, 'He is warm David, warm in bed my boy,' which meant glowing like the paraffin tin full of coals on a dark night. Therefore he always glowed, this father, red in his bed, in his imagination, warmly on the winter nights, suffusing his dreams of when he would come with the columns of a sunset sky.

Then there was the laughing. She said this so often, and with such meaning, that he knew that he also laughed in his bed, in his sleep, even when eating. So a red, glowing man, always laughing, with big hands, being a big man, and maybe covered with feathers because she said he was soft and full of love. Red, laughing, big-handed, holding love and all of this 'father', which was all right because it made up for not having an ordinary one like other children. And he was coming tomorrow, maybe to come flying this long way away, moving his feathered arms like wings as he settled in the backyard. Tomorrow was a big day all right.

After the dishes had been washed, and everything packed away in its place, and the left-overs scraped on to a piece of paper and left for the bitch, and a small piece of candle taken to the backyard room where the old woman lived, lighted and left there so that she could crawl into her blankets on the floor and sleep; when finally he had washed, his mother watching carefully, 'Behind your ears, behind your legs', and he had slipped into the old vest of hers in which he slept, then they went to bed.

They lay close together for warmth because the blankets were thin and it was the cold time of the year. There in the darkness his mother spoke again, just a little, for a while, using soft words, like live, and father and better days, and laughing; and the music in her voice made him drowsy and lapped around him like warm water as the heat from their bodies crept into the blanket. It was good to lie there like that, protected by her arms, carried away by the flow of her words which came effortless and soft, until it wasn't her voice anymore but father being just as soft, and his mother and himself were astride his back, holding on by handfuls of feathers, and all of them laughing because father was flying them away to better times, flapping his arms like a bird. The sky ahead was blue, and the sun bright and warm and lots of birds flew abreast of them and asked them where they were going and why, but they only laughed because there was no longer a need for words that weren't phrased by the sound of their happiness, and they flew like that a long time, sometimes resting up on trees, then off again, passing over strange places with strange colours, on and on, until suddenly, from nowhere, came the darkness and the sun was gone, the sky grey, and then hail, big as stones, falling hard and cruel, forcing them lower, and the stones struck his father's head with a short, dull note like hitting something iron, and this note after a slow start was going up into a frenzy of sound because the storm was at its worst, and they were going down down down ...

At that moment he opened his eyes. He shook his head in the darkness because the sound persisted in his ears. Then he noticed it was coming from the street and recognized it for what it really was. It was the sound of stones being tapped on lamp-posts. It was the warning to run away and hide because the police had come on another raid.

They were given no time to comfort or be comforted; there was not even enough for him to touch his mother and confirm that she was awake; he could feel the tenseness in her body which had been soft when they went to sleep. The door was broken open. The thin nail they had hammered into the wood and bent to hold the door closed against the wind was torn out by the first savage thrust of shoulders. As quick and as loud as this, and with as much terror, came the torch-lights. Stabbing in the dark, they found the two of them in bed, his mother on her elbows. A thin wail of terror spilt out of his lips but she gripped him by his arm, and in a strong voice said, 'No, no! David!' so he swallowed and kept quiet.

All hell had broken loose in the streets. The warning sound of the lamp-posts had either stopped or been swamped by the uproar. Voices were calling, crying, cursing; the big vans the police had come in were roaring up and down the street, their motors revving between the harsh grinding of gears and clatter and slam of the steel doors as load after load of sleepy-eyed, frightened people, caught without a pass, or just caught, were herded inside. And in the world off the street, in the intricate web of alleys and backyards that stretched back for acres on either side there in the darkness could be heard the noise of scuffling and blows as pursuer met pursued, and even more subtle, the sound of desperate and surreptitious movement as a few unfound, almost free, scuttled or crawled or clambered away into the night.

Those in his room he never saw clearly. During the few minutes they were there he caught brief glimpses of enormous khaki-coated shadows behind the torches. The one voice he heard seemed even bigger and utterly without mercy. All it said was, 'Pas kaffir.' When his mother started to speak they stretched out their hands and got her out of bed and then dragged her to the door. They were stronger than her struggles and put their boots down on her protests, and even her plea for a dress or a blanket or something warm, so that when she felt the cold air about her and saw the dark hole in the van waiting there was time only to call back, 'Don't cry, David!'.... and then she was pushed inside and the door slammed and was bolted behind her, and he was alone.

They went as soon as the vans were full. When these rolled forward the inmates crowded to the small, slatted windows on the side, hanging on to the bars and shouting back instructions to those left behind, but no one was any the wiser because all that could be heard was a desperate, urgent, hurried jumble of words: '... the police station ... two pounds ten shillings ... like last ... law-courts ... Don't cry, David ... bring food ... bring my pass ... bring money ... For gawd's sake bring money man ...'

And then they were gone. For a few moments longer voices still call loudly, doors slam, babies cry, footsteps run away in the dark, coming as a last echo to the pandemonium of a few minutes earlier. But these are separate sounds, and soon trail away and then there is silence. What follows is something like a befuddled awakening, the stirring and moaning of the survivors after a short but brutal engagement to begin a numb reckoning of losses. The destruction and looted emptiness through which they moved were not to be measured in outward things. A door hanging loose on its hinges, a broken chair, an overturned bucket of water; these were not obvious in a world made up of odd bits and pieces that never quite matched anyway. The real chaos of that moment was not to be righted or mended or filled that easily. What do you do with broken sleep, or terror, or empty blankets or the despairing prospect of a tomorrow that means your turn to search for that person, that precious person who has been taken away and might never be seen again. If you are lucky, you will find him, but then you will have to find money to help him out of the strange labyrinth of the law.

'And remember to take some food as well Sarah. Sometimes some come back after a long time and say they got no food. But where Mama, where do I go? Try here, and there and that other place as well because Lucy Mtetwa found her man there. You will wait a long time and ask many questions and if they are feeling kind that day they will fetch the big book and open it but there will be trouble because you can't spell his name and they must have the spelling of his name.'

And when they had sorted out a few things and a few thoughts, they went back to bed. No point in staying awake. Tomorrow is another day and someone else's turn to be caught. 'Why man? Why just like that, like out of the air, like lightning, any place any time? Don't you know? It's because we are defenceless. You saw them, how they came and took what they wanted and then went and we did nothing. Anything can get at us, fleas and flies in summer, rain through the roof in winter, and the cold too and things like policemen and death. It's the siege of our life, man. So what do we do?' ... Carry on. Carry on, Isaac Rabetla, Peter Madondo, Willie Sigcau, Tommy Dhlamini, you Nxumalo, Mabosos, Langas. Carry on. Tomorrow is near and your baby is crying.

He lay stiffly in bed, hardly daring to breathe, holding the edge of the blanket to his chin as if underneath it he was safe from rude hands and being hurt. This, he knew, is what he had to do. Time and again in the past his mother had unexpectedly called him, and kneeling down so that she could look straight into his eyes told him with a strange urgency in her voice what he had to do if ever it happened that she was taken away.

'Don't move, you hear. Stay in the room and wait for me there. Do you hear, David? Do you hear what I say?'

'Yes Mother.'

'What did I say?'

'I must wait for you and not move from the room.'

'Yes. Listen David. Listen carefully. Wait for me. I promise, I promise I will come back.'

He had never liked that talk but remembered it now, and so he waited. It had actually started the moment he awoke beside his mother as a total, terrible all-engulfing waiting for something to happen. When the door burst open and they came in and took her away, it became the waiting she had urged upon him, the waiting for her return. They had taken her outside, and he could hear loud voices and he wondered why they spoke to her like that and wanted to cry again but remembered her words and waited for her to come back. A little later the noise rose to a harsh, shattering climax with the vans driving away and a torrent of words from a hundred different voices, and then very quickly it subsided and most terrible of all was a deep silence with just occasionally a murmur of voices and no sound of his mother at all.

But he waited. She had said she would come back. She had promised she would come back. He strained desperately at every sound, hoping, hoping. Every time footsteps approached the room his heart beat quicker and he got ready to laugh and cry at the same time when he would hear and feel her climb back into bed, but the steps passed without stopping and he was still alone, getting lonelier with every second, feeling smaller and smaller in the bed in the darkness. Doors slammed intermittently, voices called, voices mumbled, footsteps passed in the night and then, without any warning, there was nothing more.

He waited, he ached in his waiting for the black silence to break, but nothing happened, just the dogs barked and the bitch rattled her chain and his mother didn't come.

'Mother,' he called in a resentful, hurt voice. 'Mother.' Nothing. 'Mo-ther!' – a harsh pain of a sound. His eyes were wet and his throat ached. 'M-o-t-h-e-r.'

'Tula! What is the matter?'

His surprise at getting an answer was so great that for a moment he actually thought it was his mother who had answered him. Then he heard the shuffle of footsteps crossing the yard and a scratching at the door that was like the bitch when she was a puppy and had tried to get in on cold nights.

'Will the grave be my only undisturbed rest? Is there no respect for old bones?' The match flared and by its light the old woman shuffled to the table and lit the candle. Then she turned and looked around at the empty bed, at the dress behind the door, the shoes under the bed, and lastly, searchingly, into his white, frightened eyes.

'Where is she?'

He swallowed.

'Police?' she asked.

His lips trembled, he closed his eyes.

'Mother!' It was an endless sound.

'Tula, snotnose,' the old one cried.

David crawled out of the blankets and on to his feet.

'Where do you think you are going?'

He stumbled to the door but she was quicker. An arm shot out and caught him and held him back with surprising strength. He kicked and screamed, but she held on and closing her eyes passed implacably through the frenzy of his outburst.

Reduced finally to a sobbing, weak-kneed heap of his small self, she dragged him to the bed and got him on it and under a blanket. He made no effort to get back on to his feet. While she pulled a chair to the door and sat down, he buried his face in the cold, comfortless smell of his mother in the pillow and sobbed himself to sleep.

There were no dreams. When he awoke his first impressions, the sound of a new day stirring beyond the walls of the room, the smell of woodsmoke again and the clatter of enamel mugs, the rattle of a bucket, were so much like any other day in his life that for a moment there was no memory of the night. They came with the old woman's voice.

'Are you awake?' Last night, the terror of last night! 'Do you want coffee?'

His mother! He sat up suddenly and looked around and rubbed his eyes.

'My mother. They took my mother.'

'They took your mother and the rest of the world.'

'Where is my mother?'

She shuffled up to him and held out the mug. 'Where is God in heaven! Take it.'

He dropped his head and began to sniff.

'A fine one you are,' she said. 'What sort of a man do you think you'll make?'

He didn't hear her, and anyway he wasn't going to cry. He remembered it all now, but in a numb, dull way. There were no tears in it. He was quite brave in daylight and she had said don't cry and had promised to come back. There was some sort of comfort in the old woman. She belonged in a way – to the room and his mother singing and supper in the yard. And she didn't seem worried or anything other than her usual crabby self. He drank his coffee. It was warm and there was a comfort of a sort in that too. Days were long things. There was lots of time to come back and she had promised.

The old woman was sorting herself out, fussing with an old pair of shoes and her clothing. He watched her and in between knotting the doek on her head and putting a black shawl with a fringe over her shoulders, she stopped several times and looked at him. At last she was ready and came to the bed. She spoke to him directly, in a way no big person ever did, and all the time he looked seriously and unblinkingly back into her eyes and heard everything she said.

'I'm going out.' She paused here and seemed to search his face for something. 'The last time I went out was ...' She paused again, closed her eyes momentarily and then carried on. 'I'm going out and I'll try to find her.'

'She said she would come back.'

The old woman considered this and then spoke very slowly: 'Then I'll help her. I'm taking her dress and when I meet her somewhere she'll put on her dress and be all right.'

'Can I come?'

'No. Your father is coming. You must be here.'

He heard those words like ice-cold hands in the small of his back. The old woman had turned away and was moving to the door.

'I'll try to find her if God's in heaven.'

The door closed behind her and he was alone again and as frightened as at any time in the night past. For a moment he wanted to run after the old woman but he remembered his mother's words, 'Don't move. Don't go away from the room.'

He pulled the blankets up to his chin, and started waiting again, but this time the silence was right inside himself, right deep down where his heart beat and terror lodged, moving slowly that moment like something awakening from a sleep, taking its time, flexing itself and yawning. Days are long things.

It was his father. It was the thought of his father coming here. His father coming and himself alone. It was different now. It was totally different from the homecoming his mother had talked about and he had thought about last night and all the other nights in the unending telling of the story. Then she, his mother, had been present, in his thoughts, at the moment of homecoming. His big, gentle, warm, protective mother behind whom he had ridden and escaped from the whole world of a child's fears.

That is how he had prepared himself to meet his father. Behind her. Holding on to her. Now he was alone and waiting.

He watched the passage of time in the movement of the square of sunlight from the window. He noticed that the grey fly had gone. It must have been near noon, because the sunlight had reached the table and the noise of the street had settled down to a lazy, comforting hum, and he was still alone, and still waiting heavy-eyed, when he fell asleep again.

The knocking on the door was soft but persistent. He awoke and a second later his terror sprang and caught him because unlike the first awakening he knew immediately where he was and what it was outside the door. He had put a box there to hold it closed – being too small to do anything about the nail – and when after a few more seconds of knocking a voice, a deep thundery voice, called softly: 'Tondi' and after that the box was pushed back a few inches, he clawed his way out from under the blanket and ran into the back-yard.

There, after a whimpering, desperate moment of indecision, he dived into a deserted fowl hok where he closed his eyes and his ears. But still he heard the feet walk into the room, and then the softer sound as they came a few steps into the backyard. He even heard the softer sound of a deep breath that was almost a sigh. The steps went back into the room, and then to the front door from where the voice called out, 'Tondi!' The world seemed to still itself and listen. He called a second time, 'Tondi!'

From somewhere else someone answered: 'She's gone brother.'

'Tondi?'

'Yes brother, gone. They took her this morning. The police took her this morning.'

'Tondi!'

'They took many this morning' and it was many voices answering him now, but he still only had the one word: 'Tondi!' the one name, 'Tondi!' and it was a cry now, cried with a terrible sound.

The footsteps walked about in the room, and David heard the sound of a crash and then more noise, wild breaking noise. The footsteps came into the backyard again where, loudest of all, almost in pain, he still called, 'Tondi!' until the chain rattled and he heard the snarl of the bitch and a heavy, dull sound, and a thin screech of dog pain.

'Tondi!' The steps receding, the dog screaming. 'Tondi.'

'They took her, brother.'

'I saw her without a dress.'

'Tondi! I'm come back,' receding in the distance and then heard no more; hearing now instead the bitch, which in a way was worse.

He had to open his eyes, and when he did he wished he hadn't, because for all his tears and prayers he could not close them again until it was over. He had kicked her and she was walking around in circles, biting at her own back legs and rolling over and over in the sand. She stopped and tried to stand up but she could only do so on the front ones. Her eyes were red, and her muzzle blind with pain and knowing what was coming she turned her head to the hok and started that way. She took an eternity, dragging her hindquarters which were useless in the great labour of her effort, and she was whining all the time with foam at her mouth. David shrank back, jabbering to himself, feeling for stones but finding only feathers and dry droppings and not even being able to hold these because he couldn't flex his hands.

On she came, until a foot or so away the chain stopped her, and although she pulled at this with her teeth until her breathing was tense and rattled she could go no further, so she lay down there, twisting her body so that the hindquarters fell apart and, like that, fighting all the time, her ribs heaving, she gave birth to the stillborn litter, and then died beside them.

It wasn't long before the first fly came, lit with a green sheen to his body, and a buzz that called all the others. They settled and lifted in a small black cloud, and before the day was through there were thousands and a loathsome stench, and he sat through it all, his eyes transfixed, not moving.

He runs away, tearing his hand as he breaks open the wire mesh on the side, and he runs like a little animal being hunted, very fast and very far.

It was night time and getting cold again. It might have been the same day, or the next one. He didn't know. There was no sense of time or of anything past, just the present and being somewhere he had never been before, being cold and hungry. Then he saw them trotting towards him in the darkness, keeping together like a ragged pack of mongrel beings. They stopped and watched him for a few seconds from a safe distance, and when he made no move they came up and crowded around, pulling at his clothes, pushing him provocatively from one to the other. 'Who are you?' they asked.

He looked at them blankly.

'Where do you come from?'

He had no answers.

'He one too,' someone exclaimed. 'He's like us.'

They crowded even closer and had a good look at him.

'You got a mother?' they asked.

'You got a father?'

What did they mean?

'I tell you, he is like us. Look at him. He doesn't know nothing.'

They all agreed and then their hands, instead of pulling and pummelling, began to pat him. They asked him where he was going and he said nowhere, so they said he must go with them and when he asked where that was they told him down by the river where it used to run, there by the big pipes – 'They are warm and we sleep well and we have bread and water' – showing him their crusts and bottles. One of them took his hand and led him as they trotted away happily. The pack had grown by one and now numbered eight.

On the way he noticed among other things that the oldest was a head higher than himself, while the youngest was so small he had to be carried because he was tired.

At the river there was a steep footpath down to the stony bed. Because it was new to him, he missed his footing at one point and rolled nearly all the way down, but he didn't cry. When he got up he spat and sneezed out the sand in his mouth and nose. 'You will learn,' they said. And to prove it the one who had held his hand ran quickly to the top, called to him from there, and then came running down again. 'In the dark,' he said, 'I did it in the dark.'

Then they sat down to eat and this, like everything else they did, was very serious. The bottles of water, two of them, stopped with plugs of paper, were passed around and the bread and the orange peels broken up and shared out in equal portions. The youngest, the one they had carried, caused the others great concern by not touching his food. They left off eating and drinking their own to try and urge him on. 'Eat.' 'Take it Simon.' 'Bread and peels man.' 'Dip it in your water.'

Simon wore an old coat sizes too big. When he walked it trailed behind him like a bridal gown. Now he was hidden, almost lost in its voluminous folds. He made no move to eat. So they unbuttoned the coat and the leader took out a box of matches and struck a light and they all looked at Simon's belly. It was bigger, they agreed. Bigger than yesterday because it was broader than the rest of his body and as stiff as a drum.

Simon sat through their inspection and listened to their remarks with the implacability of a small Buddha.

'Like Willie,' they said. 'He's going like Willie.'

'Who's Willie?' David asked.

'We put him away,' was the reply.

Then someone had the idea that since Willie was no more, and the new one had no name, why not call him Willie. It was an idea, they agreed, taking turns to say 'Willie' and nudge the new boy, until he also said 'Willie.' The others laughed.

After that they spoke a little about the day, and what had happened. It had been a bad day. Just bread and orange peels. They would try somewhere else tomorrow.

'Try what?' the new boy-without-a-name, the one trying to be Willie, asked.

They looked at him and were silent as if the question had no meaning.

A half-moon came up and the boy who had held his hand, on the way to the river, turned to him and said: 'You must get a bed.'

In the sharp, silvery light he led David down the riverbed and together they collected a pile of scrap-paper blown there by the wind and a few pieces of gritty cardboard.

The other boy did all the talking. 'My name is Petah. Now listen. What's the matter with you? You say nothing. Are you sleepy? I'm also too. Not long now. You'll sleep on these. I'll show you. It's all right over here, you'll see, when there's food. We'll be friends. Me and you. I'll tell you what. We must find you another name. Willie's no good man. I don't like it. It's dead, you see.'

When Petah decided they had enough papers, they went back. The others were crawling around the openings to the pipes, scurrying about on all fours like moles. Petah lead him to the last pipe.

'This is mine. You sleep with me. Are you frightened? Shall I go in first? Listen. Say something man. You say nothing.'

He showed David how to lay out the papers so that they formed a mattress. Then he crawled in, followed by David. Inside it was warm and musty and Petah's small voice boomed down the pipe, each word throbbing and yawning wide with echoes. David listened without emotion. Nothing touched him, nothing registered. He was in something like a living trance that had even made him immune to pain. And then Petah dropped off to sleep.

Framed by the opening of the pipe was a circle of smoky white sky and as he watched a small spider crawled along the inside rim and then dropped down slowly on a single thread of cobweb along which a little light danced as it swung to and fro. They were right, the other children. It was warm in the pipes. It crept into his numb body and slowly, very slowly he began to relax. Warmth. Something else, some other time, some other place had also been warm. His eyes were as heavy as leaden balls. He closed them and felt the warmth even more. It crept up his body and into his mind and there, like things frozen for all time, his thoughts began to move. Warmth. Where had it been warm? What had been warm? His pain was thawing out too. Warmth ... was a pain ... was a memory, was a pain. Something warm and soft and someone singing. All this was somewhere. Where, and who, saying what? He listened. 'Don't go.' His heart beat faster and he held his breath. The words were far away. 'Don't go. Don't move from the room ...' A tremendously urgent desperation seized him. He had to be somewhere. Some special place ... and right away. It was coming to him. He would find it. He *had* to be there or else ...

Petah awoke as he scrambled out of the pipe.

'What's it ... hey ... hey, what's your name. Willie. Where you going?'

Outside David was trying to climb up the river bank, but it was very steep and all that his efforts brought him was a cloud of dust and bleeding knees. Petah grabbed hold of him.

'What's the matter? Listen man. No, stop it now.'

The others had stuck their heads out of their pipes and were calling. When they got no answers to their questions, they rushed to Petah's assistance. Eventually they had David down on the ground.

'What's he doing?'

'He just run.'

'Hey –'

'Willie.'

'Hey Willie. What you doing?'

David looked at them, passing from face to face. He shook his head, it was gone.

'I think,' Petah said, 'I think it was home.'

They released their hold on him, and crawled back to their pipes. 'It's no good,' Petah told him. 'It's no good at night.' It was all right, he explained, to look during the day. Like with Sam. He had found his mother, but it was during the day. They all looked, in a way, during the day. But at night there was danger. Like Joji, who like him had gone home at night, but other people were living in the room, not his, and when they heard the scratching at the door they thought it was a burglar and took their sticks and beat him to death ... Joji.

'So try tomorrow ... listen.' Petah turned to David. 'Willie no good. You not Willie. What *is* your name? Talk! Trust me, man. I help you.'

David's eyes grew round and vacant, stared at the darkness. A tiny sound, a thin squeaking voice, struggled out: 'David ...' it said, 'David! But no more! He dead! He dead too, like Willie, like Joji.'

'I understand,' Petah said. 'You will choose your name. You will choose when you are ready.'

After Petah had spoken some more, and then gone to sleep, David watched the sky again through the opening. The spider came back and starting the same way, dropping down on a shiny thread, spun his web. David watched all the time. It was finished near dawn at the time of the first light in the sky and, seen through it, the morning star twinkled like a small insect caught in its trap.

He refused to go with them. They stood around and shook their heads. They coaxed him, they warned him, they even tried to threaten him, but without success. It wasn't that he argued back, or cried, or did anything at all. He just sat at the mouth of the pipe where he had slept. Nothing had much meaning for him, least of all they, seen now for the first time in the light. In their wide, unsmiling eyes and thin faces and meagre bodies was a knowledge of things beyond his experience. But he was to learn it that day, and most days after that, and learn it so well that he would never forget it, because they went and left him alone.

It started with that, loneliness, being the only person in the world, in a grey world, because clouds blew up and it rained all day. A wet, grey world smelling musty. It was the scent of damp paper; wind-blown, yellowing newspapers, and soggy cardboard and scraps. The forever afterwards mournful smell of damp paper. In a life that was only a few hours old, they, the gang, were the only memory, the only people, and he waited longingly for their return.

At the same time he learnt the lesson of his body, the lesson of hunger. Crying, or sadness, or sitting still meant hunger, and even when the only other alternative was bread and water, the alternative was still life. He hungered this way through the day, his stomach shrinking to a hard knot he held in his hand.

Petah gave him a second chance that evening when they returned and found him waiting at his pipe. 'We'll give you the bread,' he said, 'if you come tomorrow.'

He took the bread and the chance.

'Where's Simon?' he asked. No one answered. He was to learn that lesson also. The lesson about questions that had no meaning.

So he went out with them the next day and scavenged. That same day an Indian chased him away from his shop door, shouting and calling him a tsotsi. When they went back to the river that night, they started again, trying names on him: Sam, Willie, and now Simon, until he stopped them.

'My name,' he said, 'is Tsotsi.'

They crowded around him, laughing, and slapping him on the back.

'Tsotsi!' they cried, trying it out. He nodded his head.

He learnt all the lessons, he learnt them well. He never stopped learning, it seemed. Because after the river gang – broken up one night by a police raid – came other gangs of older boys, and harder, harsher lessons, and that simple lesson of keeping his body alive another day. He learned to watch for the weakness of sympathy or compassion for others weaker than yourself, like discovering how never to feel the pain you inflicted. He had no use for memories. Anyway, he had none.

$=10=$

Tsotsi opened his eyes and listened to the knocking on his door. Instinctively, but for no other reason than having awoken, he put his hand under his pillow to find his knife. Before he found it, another thought crossed his mind and he sat up on his elbows and looked down to the foot of the bed. The baby was still there, and apparently asleep.

The knocking had stopped, but now came again. Tsotsi shook his head. He must have fallen asleep, some time in the night his tiredness must have caught up with him and he had fallen asleep. No, it was in the morning. He remembered going out once to piss and hearing cocks crowing and noticing that the sky was pale. How long had he slept? He looked at the window and listened. Bright light and casual noise. Early morning.

The knocking started again. Who was that? Suddenly he thought about the woman, the one he had got to feed the baby. Why her? Why would she come back? Tsotsi shook his head again. Things were happening and thoughts were coming too fast for him. He felt for his knife, but it did exactly the opposite of what it was meant to do. Instead of pacifying him, it started a separate, new sequence of thoughts. He remembered the river again, the gangs, then his mother, then Petah ... The person outside knocked again.

'Who are you?' Tsotsi called out. The woman, could it be the woman. Why the woman? Silence. No one answering. A motor car cruised past in the street. Vague voices somewhere.

'Who is there?'

He was halfway to the door when Die Aap answered. 'Tsotsi is that you?'

Tsotsi stopped and listened.

'This is me,' Die Aap added. Jesus, what now. What the hell now. Things were happening too fast.

'What do you want?' No answer. 'Die Aap?'

'It's me. Ja. Die Aap man. Hey?'

Tsotsi gently hid the baby under the bed, before opening the door. Die Aap smiled. Where's his front teeth, Tsotsi thought, and then, why the hell am I thinking that. 'I did think you wasn't here,' Die Aap was saying.

'What's the time?'

'Morning. Can't you see?' He was still smiling.

'What do you want?' The smile went, slowly flowing away like thick oil.

Die Aap sighed at the same time, dropped his eyes and put his hands on his hips. 'Yes it's morning,' he said, ignoring the other question, 'or thereabouts.'

'What do you want?'

'I just come man.'

'For what?'

'Hell!' he whistled a few flat notes. 'Don't I just always come,' he asked eventually. 'Where else do I go. Hey? Nowhere man. I just come here.'

'Well don't.' Tsotsi closed the door in his face and went to his bed and sat down.

A few seconds later Die Aap's head appeared at the window. He tried to whistle again but gave it up. 'Why?' he asked.

Tsotsi repeated the question for him. 'Yes why.'

My mother, he thought. My father. The bitch. The river. A spider spinning a web – but most of all my mother. He had to return to that thought. Everything started there. It was the beginning of himself, and of his memories, spinning like silk thread out of the soft shimmer of her humming on a day long, long forgotten. Was it true? Was it really true, had it been him? 'My mother,' he said aloud. The words were strong, and full of meaning and a clear image formed in his mind.

Had he looked he would have seen Die Aap's eyes widen at the window. There was a thought if ever there was one. Tsotsi's mother!

'Your mother. Mine is dead.'

'You knew her.'

'Not yours. Mine. She died.'

Tsotsi looked at Die Aap. It was strange. He had never realized it before. Every man had a mother. Every single person in the world had a mother. Boston too. (Jesus, what about Boston. He would get around to that.) And Die Aap ... and Butcher.

'Where is Butcher?'

'Gone. He won't come.' Die Aap was resting his chin on the windowsill. His head bobbed as he spoke. 'But I did.'

Tsotsi considered this. Butcher gone. Boston gone. The gang finished. Just like that. Finished. Himself thinking it just like that. One word. Finished. What now? Another gang? Could there be another one? Why not . . . Since the river . . . But what about before the river?

'He was fed up about Saturday,' Die Aap continued. 'He said you done a job alone.' Saturday night and the cripple. 'We come here on Sunday morning but you wasn't here.' Sunday morning and the ants. 'We come back in the afternoon but we heard a woman here.' The woman who had fed the baby.

'Ja. Maybe you did!' Tsotsi said suddenly. 'Maybe there was a woman here. Maybe I done a job alone. So what?'

'That's what I tell him Tsotsi. All along I been saying maybe. And when he says this morning to let us go join up with Buster and his boys I says maybe but he finds a bloody long word man and goes.'

'So what are you doing here?'

'I come here.'

'Why don't you go with him?'

'Two years Tsotsi.'

'What's two years?'

'We been together.'

Tsotsi looked at Die Aap. He blinked a few times as if that would clear his vision of habit, of the muzziness that came from seeing the same thing so much until you saw it no more. Two years and he's got no front teeth and . . . two years . . . strong . . . the strongest . . . two years he stayed and followed me like a dog follows a man.

'So we start again Tsotsi, hey man. It was like this then. So now we find a couple of others and we start again and . . .'

The baby started crying.

For a moment Die Aap was fooled and he looked back over his shoulder. Then he realized the sound was coming from the room, from under the bed on which Tsotsi was sitting. He opened his mouth to say something and then realized that Tsotsi hadn't moved when it started, hadn't even registered that he'd heard the sound. Just sitting there watching him. Die Aap closed his mouth, and pretended he hadn't heard a thing.

It cried for a few minutes. Die Aap tried to whistle again; looked up at the ceiling, the floor; then all the walls. Tsotsi was thinking, start again, since the river ... but what about before the river?

The baby stopped suddenly. 'No Aap. You're wrong. We don't start again.'

'No.'

'It's finished.'

'Me ...'

'Finished man. Like breakfast, or yesterday or Boston. Finished cold.'

'So what do I do?'

'Go.'

'Where?'

'I don't care.'

'Okay.'

He waited a few minutes longer and in that time they stared at each other. Once more Die Aap tried to whistle, but failed.

Then he left, neither having said another word. Tsotsi went to the window and watched him walk down the street. He looks drunk, he thought. He walks drunk. What do I care? He had said finished. What did that mean? What was finished, like breakfast and yesterday and Boston? Maybe he was dead. Jesus, what about Boston — maybe he, Tsotsi, would be too late. Wait, wait man. His time is coming, is near. Finished? ... with songs? What else was there? What else had there ever been? Only one day a long, long time ago before the river. But what the hell was finished? He had said it, he had said it himself.

The baby cried again. Tsotsi went back and brought it out from under the bed. For the first time since the night in the grove of bluegum trees, when fate forced it into his hands, he was glad he had it. He rejoiced in the very things that had disgusted and angered him in the past, like its smell, its wizened ugliness, its crying the raucous yell of noise that came unendingly out of its black hole of a mouth. Everything about it that touched, or could be touched by one of his senses gave him satisfaction. This was reality, to be heard, to be felt, to be smelt. This was no phantom from his past that came like a dream remembered after many years and yet ... and yet *seemed* real. He could hold the baby in his hands. It was real now, and it was the beginning of three strange days and it was still with him and crying and wanting milk and things. Its function that moment went beyond giving him a hold on an actual moment of the living, urgent present. He had become the repository of Tsotsi's past. The baby and David, himself that is, at first confused, had now merged into one and the same person. The police raid, the river, and Petah, the spider spinning his web, the grey day and the smell of damp newspapers were a future awaiting the baby. It was outside itself. He could sympathize with it in its defencelessness against the terrible events awaiting it.

Not irrelevantly – because despite the woman's visit the baby looked worse than ever – he thought of death. What if it died? Then he, Tsotsi, would have to take the past back and what could he do with it? What could he, in his life, in that room, do with a day a long, long time ago and a woman humming and a little boy happy with cotton reels on the floor?

'Stay alive,' he said aloud. 'Stay alive – David. I'll get you mother's milk.'

When some time later Miriam Ngidi took her place in the water queue, Tsotsi was waiting at his window, standing so that he could watch her without being seen. He noticed that she looked back at his room many times and he wondered if it meant that it was going to be easier to get her. He decided that it did, because there wasn't much fear in the way she moved or in her face when she looked back. It was a furtive, quick turn of the head when she bent to pick up her bucket and move a few steps forward. After each look she lapsed into an absent mood and seemed to think deep and not to notice anything around her. Then it was her turn at the tap, and when her bucket was full she started on the way back.

Tsotsi had also had time to notice many other things that he had missed the previous day, like the strong slant to her eyes, and the ochre tint of her skin, which was not black like most of the others'. She stood straight and, although not very tall, she looked it because of the way she carried her body, walking well, with a full roll of her hips. One baby had not marked her, or if anything only turned a girl into a woman; the moment of ripening, they said in the township. You only speak of a tree after picking the first fruit.

When she was still a distance away he left the window and went to the door, opening and stepping outside, and then just standing there where she could see him. She came a few more steps and pretended to be tired, putting down her bucket. She wasted a few more seconds by fiddling with the blanket that held the baby to her back, bending forward from the waist while doing so. It was in this position, with a safety pin between her white teeth, that she looked up suddenly and Tsotsi caught her eye.

He held it longer and looked deeper than he had done with anyone else in his life, making sure in that time that she understood that his baby was waiting in the room again and that he was asking her. He waited for her to pick up her bucket and start walking. When she had come to within a few steps of him, he turned and went into the room.

He wasn't sure she had followed until the room darkened, and then he knew that she was in the doorway. Even so he did not look back but went straight to the bed. 'He's been crying,' he said. 'He looks bad. I got nothing for him. You will feed him again.'

Silhouetted in the door, with the light behind her, he could see nothing of her face. He didn't need to. The hesitation was obvious and he was about to say something else, something maybe about her baby that would make her decide when she finally came in and closed the door. After the glare it took him a few seconds to accustom his eyes to the dark. When he could see her clearly, she was already at the bed, loosening the blanket that held her child.

He knew then that she had wanted to come, that she had come prepared to come; that for all he knew she might even have knocked on his door in passing if he had not stepped out into the street. He knew that first because of the ointment she smeared around the sore lips, dipping her finger into a small jar that had come out of a pocket in her dress. There were also the clean clothes come out of the blanket to clothe it, and the powder she dusted all over the small baby. In all this, the ointment, the washing and the clothing, her own baby cried once, but she silenced it with soft words, bending low so that it could smell her presence.

Then she unbuttoned her blouse; it was the same one with the buttons sewn on again, and she started feeding and this he watched intently because he had not seen it the first time. Her breasts were big and full of milk and they started dripping even before she had a nipple in the small mouth. The baby gave her trouble. After sucking for a few seconds with a loud greedy noise, he then turned his head and the milk dribbled out of the corner of his mouth.

She bounced him for a few seconds on her lap, rubbing his back all the time, and then tried again. The same thing happened.

'Little one! What is the matter? You must drink. Look at you, ai siestog. Just look. What is your name? Drink my baby. What will we call you? Peter. The big fisherman. Drink Petertjie.'

'His name is David.'

Miriam looked at Tsotsi. 'Are you his father?'

His father! A big, feathered man, flying them away to better times. Ow, David, he thought. Poor David. There were no better times. Just the river. Tsotsi closed his eyes. 'David,' he said, and he was shocked to hear the hard sound of the words, 'never saw his father.'

Miriam clicked out her sympathy. Anyway, she knew his real name now and could speak to him. Tsotsi listened. They weren't words – just sounds, soft woman sounds that took him back again ... His mother, what the hell does a man do with a mother? Was it really so? Had it really been him?

'Give him to me.' The baby was drinking deeply.

He caught his breath and waited. It was the woman speaking.

'Give him to me. He is sick. Give him to me and I will take him and look after him.'

He thought of his knife first. I will kill her. Here in this room. She and her child. I will kill them fucking dead.

'I can feed it,' she was saying, 'I have good milk. I know about babies.'

Then he thought about the baby. I gave him milk. Me on a Saturday in a shop, I bought it. I killed the ants.

The woman spoke on. 'You can see him, you can come to my room and see him and he will get big and strong like my child. They will play together, Simon and David. Give him to me.'

A long time passed like that. He never spoke and she only once, to the baby, when she changed to the other breast.

'It's empty,' he thought. 'One tit is empty.'

Then he drifted off into his own thoughts again. He remembered the river, he always returned to the river. For all its being dry and littered with rubbish, it flowed unceasingly through his mind because it was the beginning. They had played one game. It was the game of the rusty shell of the old motor car that had crashed into the river one night, and by their time had been stripped clean so that all that remained was the frame, gaping, socketed, like a skull. The game was called driving to hell and gone. It was intricate to play and involved filling up with petrol and water, testing the tyres and oil, loading the luggage in the boot and then all climbing in and driving away very fast. The best part was being the driver, and they took turns at that:

> *beep-beep, toot-toot,*
> *Grrr-grrr-grrrrrrr ...*

Somehow they had always seemed to play it late in the afternoon in the fading light. The rule was that only the driver made the noises. The rest sat silent while he raced the gloom of evening which always fell first there in the riverbed.

> *Beep-beep,*
> *Grr-grr-grrrrrrr.*

There was an uncanny sensation of speed and danger as darkness settled and the shadows lengthened and the others held their breath, running away to hell and gone.

Mistaking Tsotsi's silence for consideration, Miriam spoke on. 'He needs milk. He needs it more than you think. I'm telling you this boy David is sick. He may die. What do you know? But I will take him because yesterday I was jealous about my milk and it was wrong and feeding him makes me happy.'

Tsotsi wasn't hearing her anymore. She gave him to me, under the trees. She gave to me. Nobody can take him away. He is mine, he is mine!

She had put the baby down on the bed beside hers and was standing open. Her blouse hung open. In her excitement she had forgotten her modesty.

'Look at them. I'll tell you something. Last night I was sad and I bent on my knees and did pray for something and a voice said, Why should I give you what you ask me for, when you got no milk for babies. Please give him to me.'

'He is *mine*,' Tsotsi finally said, glad that the words came so easily and did not fall over each other in their hurry to get out.

'But you are not his father,' she said.

'He is *mine*.' There was no arguing with the finality in his voice, yet for a long time Miriam remained standing at the table, bent slightly forward so as to see Tsotsi clearly.

'He is *mine*,' he said again and then she moved, dropping her head first, then going back to the bed, where she sat, righted her blouse and watched the sleeping babies.

'Where did you get him?'

'He was given to *me*,' he said.

'Where?' she asked, impatient with his insistence.

'Under the trees.'

'And the mother?'

'She ran away in the night.'

The woman looked at him, a frown between her eyes.

'She ran away in the night,' he said, making his words as big as he could, shaping them massively with his hands as they came out. 'She didn't cry for him. She didn't give him no milk. She just got him in a box and she gave him to me and she just ran away in the night.'

'Tell me,' the woman said.

'I just told you.'

'Tell me more,' she insisted.

So he started again, from the beginning, telling some things many times until he remembered something else, Miriam listening through it all with a frown and patience, telling without shame how he had seen her coming through the night with the box, and had waited for her, and how he was left holding the baby. He stopped there, because what followed was still beyond words, and of no interest to her.

'When did it happen?' she asked.

He counted back the days. 'Three.' She shook her head and clicked her tongue softly, so he went on about the milk and feeding it and the ants.

She was watching him carefully when he reached the end. His eyes were excited and his hands trembling because never before had he spoken so many words at once.

'What are you going to do with him?'

'Keep him.'

'Why?'

He threw back his head, and she saw the shine of desperation on his forehead as he struggled with the one mighty word. Why, why was he? No more revenge. No more hate. The riddle of the yellow bitch was solved – all of this in a few days and in as short a time the hold on his life by the blind, black, minute hands had grown tighter. Why? 'Because I must find out,' he said.

She considered this, but finding her thoughts going around in a circle she turned to the baby again. She uncovered a medicine bottle of milk in her blanket and put it on the table.

'Give him this tomorrow,' she said, 'with a spoon. I will come in the afternoon at the same time.'

Then it was the business again with the blanket, and her own

baby with a safety pin between her teeth. She straightened, picked
up her bucket and went to the door.

'Tomorrow,' he said.

'Tomorrow –' and she went out.

He gave her time enough to reach her room, and then he picked
up the baby and slipped out into the street, and then up to the ruins,
but even so he looked back twice on the way in case she had hidden
somewhere and was following him.

After hiding the baby, he set off purposefully in the opposite
direction from which he had come. It was a long walk and took him
right through the township, reaching his destination towards the
middle of the afternoon. Tsotsi found he couldn't control himself.
His heart raced and strange sounds broke from his lips as he ran
down the footpath to the bottom of the river.

It was true. The pipes were exactly as he remembered them,
choked with dry leaves and sand now, smelling rusty. The only
change was that more rubbish seemed to have been thrown or
blown into the riverbed. He hurried down it. When he found the
shell of a motor car, almost as he remembered it, there was no
longer any doubt. It was true, it had happened, and to him.

He didn't stay a second longer than was necessary, almost
running in his hurry to leave the river. Once he got back among
the houses and people, he slowed down. It was dark when he
reached his street and he slipped into the first shebeen to ask after
the whereabouts of Boston.

$$=11=$$

Tsotsi finally traced Boston to a shebeen bossed by a woman called
Marty. Boston had found himself there shirtless, shoeless, wearing
only an old pair of khaki trousers held up by a belt of fibrous yellow
rope. He was lying in a corner of the room on the floor, lost to the
world in a stupor which had lasted now for the three days that had
passed since Tsotsi's attack, and out of which he had awoken at
times, only to lurch off in search of still more booze. Spit bubbles

burst as he breathed through his lips because his nose was blocked with blood.

Tsotsi came just in time. As he slipped quietly to the door, the woman, Marty, was standing over Boston, nudging him with her foot and speaking in a deep, disgusted voice. 'Hey! Hey! Wake up. Wake up and get out man. I'm sick of you, bloody dog.'

The other occupants of the room, two men, were watching idly over their drinks.

'Throw him out,' she said. 'Throw him out the bloody dog. He's pissed again on the floor.'

No one had seen Tsotsi in the door, with the result that when he spoke there was an immediate reaction. Marty swung round, and the men made a quick move to hide their glasses. 'Leave him,' said Tsotsi.

'What do you want?' she asked.

'Him' – nodding his head at Boston.

Marty left the corner and walked right up to Tsotsi, standing so that she blocked his way. She didn't fear a damn thing.

'You're the one that did it,' she said.

Tsotsi had nothing to say in reply.

'You worked him like he is. Lying down, he said. When he couldn't see because the blood was in his eyes.'

Tsotsi waited for her to finish. He looked over her shoulder at the men, who dropped their eyes, then at the ceiling where a piece of flypaper crusted over with dead bodies hung beside the light.

Marty had come so close to him that when she spoke small drops of spit flew into his face. 'I wouldn't do that to a dog. Not to a mad dog and I'm telling you he was a man. So what you got to say?'

She waited. Tsotsi waited.

'I'm telling you, that,' she pointed back but without taking her bright, indignant eyes from Tsotsi's face, 'that was a man. I know. Some sort of a different man – Well?'

'I want him.'

'Why? Aren't you satisfied?'

'I just want him – to talk.'

The light faded from her eyes. 'To talk! Ja ja, he could talk, too much.'

Marty walked away from him, a big, childless, husbandless woman. At the table she lit a cigarette, smoked it for a few seconds, blowing on the glowing tip of the cigarette. She looked at Boston once, and then shrugged her shoulders.

'Take him. It's too late. He shouldn't have come back.'

Tsotsi tried to wake Boston at first, but after the shaking he just rolled over. The two men watched discreetly, dropping their eyes to their glasses whenever Tsotsi caught them. Marty was at her window, leaning there on her elbows, looking out into the night.

'He's just pieces,' she said. 'Just pieces held together by dried blood, like something broken.'

Boston stank as bad as a backyard. He had also messed in his trousers.

'Who wants pieces?' Marty was saying. 'Who the hell wants the pieces of a man?'

Tsotsi carried him away in his arms.

It took him a long time to get back to his room. At first Boston was quiet, and apart from the weight, it was easy going through the crooked streets, past the idle curiosity of people waiting at their windows for another rain, or lounging about outside. What's that mean, they asked themselves and each other. That man there, hey! Carrying that one like a baby. They knew the basic meaning: trouble. That was the meaning of most things. But the form of it, the variations that life composed, playing on that one theme, they were infinite. Was it brother, father or friend? Was he alive, dead or dying? Who did it, anyway, and why? What exactly had been done?

About halfway to his room, Boston awoke. Tsotsi heard him groan. But it was only when they reached the light of a lamp-post that he knew for certain he was awake. One eye was open wide and staring back. When Boston saw who it was that carried him, he gave a small cry, and with a flurry of legs and arms broke loose and fell to the ground. He staggered up and went lurching away into the darkness, still crying in a strong nasal tone, because of his blocked nose.

Tsotsi followed him as he stumbled, off the pavement and into the gutter, then on the pavement again, but now on his knees because he had fallen over the kerb; finally crawling a few more yards until he came to rest under a corrugated iron fence. There was a slogan on it: WE WON'T MOVE.

But Boston did, a few seconds later. Tsotsi pulled him to his feet, and because he was awake took one of his arms over his shoulders and helped him like that along another stretch of the way to his room. He lost consciousness again and had to be carried for the last few blocks.

In his room Tsotsi lay Boston on the bed, took off his trousers and threw them into the yard where the small dog found them later. He turned away from the window and stopped immediately, drawing in his breath with excitement. He had lit a candle on first entering the room and by its willowy light and the perspective of a few feet he now saw all that there was of Boston, stretched naked on the bed. In the shebeen and when carrying him through the streets, he had deliberately deferred the moment of looking, of really looking at him so that through the touch of his hands and his eyes he would feel him the way he had felt the cripple. But this time there was no preamble to the experience.

As he turned away from the window it hit him. Boston was thinner than he had ever imagined. His ribs stood out clearly, pressing against the skin with the effort of each breath, which seemed to arch his body. In the uncertain light his legs were out of all proportion to the rest of him. Tsotsi went to the bed and examined him carefully, so absorbed in his purpose that he hardly felt the liquid wax fall on to the back of the hand holding the candle.

The head was almost misshapen by blue swellings on the forehead. One eye was so swollen that all that remained of it was a straight fold of skin. Even as Tsotsi looked, a few drops of colourless liquid oozed out and trickled down the cheek. Impulsively he put out his hand and caught up one on his finger. He tasted it. Tears. Tsotsi straightened up and scratched off the candle wax on the back of his hand. He was trembling. He bent down again. From the eyes he moved slowly to the nose – a clotted mass of blood and broken bone – then to the mouth and the cuts about the chin. Very lightly he put a hand on Boston's chest. The flesh was warm and living and felt like pain. It was as red as pain, too, where he had broken it open.

Tsotsi straightened up again and went to the table where he put the candle down. His head was spinning. He'd held his breath during the examination and now his heart raced and his stomach was convulsing. Tsotsi sat down and waited for the dizziness and nausea to pass.

Then he counted his money. Two shillings. What did he expect after three days without a job. Two shillings. It would buy a loaf of bread and a tin of sourmilk. He blew out the candle and left the room. It took ten minutes to buy the food. When he returned he struck a match and had another look at Boston. He hadn't moved.

Tsotsi sat down in the dark. I won't light the candle, he thought. It's short. I'll need it when he talks. He ate some of the bread, drank half the milk, and waited.

Walter 'Boston' Nguza. Born at Umtata, the son of a humble, tired old woman. Educated there to standard eight at St John's College. Promising pupil, nearly always first in his class. Mother very proud. Scholarship to St Peter's High School, Johannesburg. At this period a small, shrunken youth with spectacles. Too serious. No luck with the girls. Then the training college for teachers. Again a scholarship. Mother, older, but very proud. At the end of his first year, having studied until he was almost a wreck, Walter Nguza came first in his class. 'A man with a future.' 'You'll go far Nguza.' 'Serve your people, etc.' Mother very proud.

The second year, after a loss of appetite and another supreme effort, again head of his class. 'Take it easy, Boston Boy. You'll go off the rails man.' Still shrunken, still wearing glasses, still no progress with the girls. But his mother very, very proud. Third and final year. He never wrote the final examinations for the diploma because in June that year he was expelled for trying to rape a fellow student.

Once, in the years that followed the warm, storm-expectant highveld night in June – he was twenty-four years old as he lay on Tsotsi's bed – Boston had during an idle moment written down this summary of his early career. He was proud of it. Simple, concise, no sentiment, no unnecessary detail; the straight, rising line of a life – of a hungry boy, a lonely youth, a desperate young man – rising in a clean curve to the point where it broke. The precise spot was a grove of trees near the college tennis courts at ten o'clock on that June night.

He had read it out once to a bunch of the boys.

'Go on,' they said when he was finished. He blinked at them. He had already given up wearing glasses. In some ways and for some things it was better not to see.

'Go on,' they said. 'What happened?'

'There is nothing more to tell.'

'Afterwards.'

'There is nothing more to tell. It all ended that night.'

'Ja.'

'It's all finished. Everything. Finished as dead as cigarette ash.'

'Tell about the girl then.'

'What is there to tell?'

'You tried your luck with her?'

'Ja.'

'Just like that.'

'Ja.'

. . . That was one story Boston could not spin out, not even during the long afternoons in Tsotsi's room, waiting there with him and Butcher and Die Aap for darkness. In the years that had passed he'd tried only once.

'I didn't do it. I tell you I didn't – not the way they thought I did. I was out walking. Hell, I remember. I was sick of the books and scared. You believe that. I was already scared of the exams. It was a warm night. I'm telling you, that sort of night still gives me creeps under my skin. Near the tennis courts I bumped into this girl. She was also a student. Like I was telling you, I never had any luck with the girls. It had got so bad I was scared of them. When I saw her there I wanted to run. But she started to talk. What could I do? What did I know about what she had in her mind. You see, she just wanted to play, but I tell you I had no luck with the girls. So when she came near me and started rubbing. Hell! Was that a hot night. You see I didn't know when to stop. I didn't know that you went just so far and no further. She started screaming and they came running and found me. She was all in tears. But I mean, what could I do? What could I say? That's how it happened.'

Could you now honestly say he was to blame? Or the girl for that matter? And the others? The stern-faced, the disappointed, the shocked ('Nguza! No!'), they had come running only when it was already over. His mother? There was a thought there. But in the end it didn't matter who was to blame because it came down to the same thing: Walter Nguza packing his few things and leaving the college, saying to himself, numbly, 'It's a mistake.' That was putting it in a nutshell. A mistake. Couldn't really even call it an injustice.

Since then he'd had an obsession with mistakes and seen so many of them – for some men even died, like that fool Gumboot – that in his twenty-fourth year he had finally arrived at what he called the philosophy of error. 'It's a mistake,' he said when he was drunk, which was the time when he saw it clearest. 'The whole bloody thing, from beginning to end, from Adam to Walter Boston Nguza is one big mistake. No kidding.'

He went straight from the college to the railway station and spent his whole day there waiting for the train. Had it been a morning train he might have avoided the biggest mistake of all, not going home, because that is what happened. He was given too much time to brood on the image of a tired, getting-old, very proud woman hoeing in the fields. He could see her shield her eyes from the sun and look down the road, and seeing him, come running to the hut to meet him. 'Mother ...' He went no further. It was too painful.

With himself Boston was honest, but to his mother he lied. In the corner of the platform where he sat, he said aloud: 'I don't have enough courage,' and then took out a sheet of paper and wrote back home. Dear mother. Good weather. Healthy boy. Missing her. He'd finished his studying earlier than expected and so was going to look for a post up here. It would take time. Be patient! SO DON'T LET MR MABUSA WRITE YOUR LETTERS TO THE COLLEGE. I'M NOT THERE ANY MORE. Would let her have an address soon. Everything fine.

He put it into an envelope, addressed it, then threw away his ticket and hurried out of the station building. Carrying his suitcases he wandered aimlessly through the city, sleeping at night wherever he could find shelter; waiting for some miracle to sort out the mess he'd made of his life. A week was spent like this, and all that Boston subsequently remembered of it was the moment at the very end when he discovered that the last of his money was gone and he was hungry.

Fate stepped in and took over when he was on the verge of surrendering himself to the disgrace he had tried to avoid in not going home. Johnboy Lethetwa. He would always remember that name, because, although they had tried to bluff themselves, that was the beginning. Johnboy Lethetwa. The place where they had met was even more distinct because that was still there, whereas Johnboy had passed away like so many others since him.

It happened at the Pass Office, and the time, ten o'clock on a cold winter's morning. He had ended up there because a distant, a vaguely distant relative was supposed to work there, and if blood ties meant anything the man might be prepared to help. He had taken up a position near the fence, sitting on his two suitcases. There was a lot to think about before he found him, like the basic issue of Do! or Don't! If he did, would the news get back to his mother? The relative was bound to ask questions. Even if he didn't, what did he, Boston, expect from the man? Money? Food? A place to sleep? Work?

Boston looked around. It was certainly the right place to evaluate his bleak needs and prospects. The centre of all interest was the pass offices themselves, a collection of squat, ugly, rambling barrack-type buildings, a hangover from the great war that had raged in his youth, but somewhere else, broken down and reassembled here. The building stood in the centre of a windswept, barren piece of land. They had tried to grow flowers once. Two elderly black men had laid out the bed, and planted flowers, and watered them, only to watch them grow a little and then shrivel and die. 'It's too salt,' they had said, looking at each other and knowing what they meant. 'The soil is too salt over here.' So on head office's suggestion the neat diamonds and ovals and border strips of the bed had been filled with white gravel.

Outside these white, glaring patches, the earth was bare. It was kept permanently free of weeds by the thousands of feet that tramped there hopelessly each day. Along the perimeter of the grounds was a high fence, and beyond that a pavement with a little grass, where men and women sat out the lunch hours with packets of chips bought from an Indian shop across the road, waiting for the offices to open and another adventure in the intricacies of Native Administration.

The grass was a dry burnt brown around Walter Boston Nguza, sitting on his suitcases, and there were white patches of frost from the previous evening.

The man strolled up and sat on the grass beside him. He was short, stockily built, with humour in his eyes. They exchanged a few pleasantries before the stranger said: 'I see by your glasses that you are a reading man.' Boston nodded. The other one thereupon handed him a slip of paper he had in his hand: 'What does that say?' he asked.

Boston read it. 'It says you can't work at Natty Outfitters because your last employer did not sign your book.'

Johnboy Lethetwa took back the paper and nodded his head. 'That's what I thought.'

'What's it mean?'

'They'll pick me up. Ja.'

'Why didn't he sign it?' Boston asked.

'I was in jail,' Johnboy said.

'Why?'

'For not having a previous employer.'

'Let me see your pass.'

Johnboy gave it to him. This was the sort of problem that had always put him head of his class. Words on paper. He read it carefully, the instructions, then taking out a pen he signed his name, with appropriate date, then time. He handed it back to Johnboy.

'There. You've got a previous employer,' he said.

'Is that a fact,' murmured the other. He examined it carefully before putting it away. He stood up and walked away into the crowd.

Thinking he had seen the last of him, Boston considered his problem again and decided it would be best if he found his relative to inquire about work. If the man was a gentleman he himself would suggest food. Boston stood up, and was on the point of leaving when he saw Johnboy. He was walking slowly towards him, kicking a few stones and practising soccer passes. He sat down in the same position, looked around very carefully, then took four passbooks out of his pocket and handed them to Boston.

'Previous employers,' he said.

Boston took the passbooks, but hesitated. In the meantime Johnboy had taken four ten-shilling notes out of another pocket. He separated two and gave them quietly to Boston.

'Fifty-fifty,' he said.

Boston took the passes and signed them all.

The next time Johnboy brought seven, then four, finally two.

'I think we'd better stop now,' Johnboy said. 'They're beginning to look at me. Let's go and eat.'

It was twelve o'clock and Boston had over four pounds in his pocket. Johnboy picked up one of his suitcases and started walking. Boston took the other and followed him.

'What about Natty Outfitters?' Boston asked.

'To hell with them,' Johnboy said, dribbling a stone with his feet. 'We'll specialize in previous employers. Where do you stay?'

'Nowhere.'

'You can sleep with me. I got room in the hostel. Do you like soccer? I play every Saturday.'

That night Boston wrote to his mother again. As you can see from the attached pound note I am quite happy and have every hope for the future. Health good, miss you, good friend Mr J. Lethetwa where you can get Mr Mabusa to compose letter for you and send them to me.

Johnboy and Boston prospered and went a long way together. From the proceeds of previous employers they eventually saved enough to buy a few rubber stamps from one of the clerks in the Pass Office and so expanded their business to include work-seekers' permits, the forty-eight-hour visitors' permit and a small but lucrative sideline of residence permits for one of the townships. Those stamps, together with an inking pad, which the clerk also sold them, Boston carried in his raincoat pocket.

They set up shop wherever the people gathered, like the railway station, the bus terminus, the Pass Office, Johnboy collecting the customers and Boston handling the books and papers. Letters from his mother, written by the shopkeeper, Mr Mabusa, began to arrive at his new address, full of gratitude for the money and hope for the future and when are you coming home? He answered faithfully, and sent her money.

Their partnership was only in business. Beyond that they had nothing in common. Boston didn't mind. He had a lot to think about and the shebeens were as good a place as any to brood about the old mistakes and the new ones, his own, or those of other people that he had seen. When he wasn't thinking, drinking helped to pass the time and keep his hands busy. He took to it naturally, not noticing what was happening until he was deep and well-soaked in the habit. The long nights with nothing to do, a man with few friends and no luck with the girls. Johnboy went his own way. Boston stayed on the fringes, you might say, within touching distance of the real thing.

There was a gang which frequented the same shebeen; he heard their talk and sometimes added a word of his own. Their real meeting place was Marty's and he was a frequent visitor. So when a day came when Johnboy did not return, and he got the word that he had been picked up with ten passbooks in his pocket, it was the end to that game – he was not really worried. That night in Marty's, sitting alone in a corner with a glass in his hand, he heard those three men discuss a job. They had a problem and were discussing it. It was a simple problem, the solution even simpler, so simple that they were amazed when Boston pointed it out to them. They looked at him with disbelief, while Marty laughed. They gave him a cut, of course, and that was the beginning of the real thing. Before long he was going out with them on jobs.

And the letters kept coming from home. They were soul-searching, longing letters and their loneliness and ignorance of the real nature of things, phrased awkwardly in Mr Mabusa's stilted language, was as corrosive as acid to his peace of mind. We live in the hope of your return and pray for the future ... Should your career bring you to near our humble world, please ... My son, will my eyes behold my flesh and blood before I die ...

Once in desperation he dragged off the best-looking member of the gang; they dressed neatly and had their photograph taken together by a street photographer. 'Smile up, gents,' he said. Boston sent it home. Dear Mother. I thought you might like to meet another teacher who is a friend of mine. His name is Butcher Songile and we are good friends, etc.

In his own world Boston was the man with the brain, but also a coward who got sick and then drank for days after a rough job. But he was a gentleman, Please, and Thank you, and May I, and Would you like me to? That counted for a lot in Marty's eyes. Over a long time and almost unnoticed, they grew very close to each other. Other men came and went in her life, and after each departure he was still there in his corner with his drink and wry smile, with a word about this or that, ready to listen if she wanted to speak, talking on long after the others had gone, staying there into the early hours – until the day he did not leave at all. He evoked a deep, frustrated maternal impulse in her nature; his very clumsiness, his strange attempts at physical cruelty in the act, and the next morning remorse, those were the very things that held her.

It ended very abruptly, and a lot more started because of the first killing. The victim was the night watchman of the block of flats, and if they hadn't killed him they would certainly have been caught, so there was that much to be said about it. But Boston got sick; it was the smell and feel of blood. And from his stomach the nausea went to his mind. Back in the shebeen he tried to vomit out his muck and misery of his past years in a torrent of words. One drink too many, too blinded to know what he was doing, he had turned on Marty and dragged her down as low as his words.

Marty had taught him all he was ever to know about love; it began as a friendship and ended as a strange, warm interlude that had no precedent and was to have no real sequel in his lonely life. But she became part of his degradation and he was sick – sick to his soul. She took it without flinching, and because there was so much between them she let it pass without taking any of the cruel or hard revenge she was capable of.

Boston regretted having done it, because in those long years

Marty was the nearest he had found to something good, and it was finished. The police turned on the pressure, then, and the gang broke up and for a long time he didn't go near her place. When eventually he did chance his arm one day, it was to be served coldly like the others, coldly, kept at a distance as if nothing had ever passed between them, neither love nor hate. That hurt more than anything else she could have done to him. He kept away again, and two years passed before that night two days after Tsotsi had beaten him down.

Boston awoke at the darkest hour of the night.

Sitting in his chair, waiting for him, Tsotsi had heard the time pass as a sequence of sound, starting with early night, the music and laughing, and through that to a time when the laughing had stopped, and then still later the music as well, voices mumbling then in sleepy accents, and then almost at the end the occasional, defiant revels of the last one, sudden voices that were shouting until they too passed and at the last there was silence.

The bed creaked, and then Boston asked aloud in the darkness: 'Where am I?'

Tsotsi left his chair and lit the candle. The two men looked at each other in the wan light. For a moment, for the smallest, blinked fraction of the silence that passed as they eyed each other, there was fear in Boston. Then the defeat, the total and final defeat of his body, of himself, of his manhood, was remembered and he cared no longer and his fear passed. He closed his eyes and Tsotsi went back to his seat. It was better with his eyes closed. There were no irrelevances like other faces, or objects or colour – just his pain.

'Why did you bring me here?' he asked.

'I need to speak with you,' Tsotsi said.

If it had been the Boston of any other time, he would have sat up rigid in the bed, his eyes bright with excitement. Now he was no longer interested. All that had happened was too total, too final and complete for him to retrace his steps back to some point along the way where he had still been stumbling to this moment.

'Have you seen me?'

'Ja.'

'You did it.'

A long silence and then Tsotsi replied: 'I felt you.'

What is he trying to say? That he felt for me, Tsotsi? A flicker of interest, so he opened his eyes and stared, and then a second later closed them again. What did it matter?

'My youth,' Boston said, saying it because he found the phrase on his lips, saying it because in the broken, shattered days that had passed since Tsotsi's attack it had been in his mind constantly, evocative, charged with nostalgic pain. It had a meaning he couldn't even explain to himself.

Tsotsi tried again. 'I need to know things, Boston man.'

Boston listened in silence.

'I need to know things. You must tell me.'

'Why me?'

'You were a teacher man. You read the books.'

Boston looked at Tsotsi carefully. Was it the light, was it his eyes? There were lights in those eyes. Where there had been darkness there was something like light. The effort tired him out. He closed his eyes. 'I know nothing.'

And Tsotsi, not knowing the nature of the ignorance the other man confessed, said, 'I'll tell you.'

First of all, he told him about the baby, and Boston listened for a long time, piecing together the broken sentences, the half-thoughts of the other man, until he had the picture. Tsotsi and a baby, that was a strange thought – could it be true? Why not, Tsotsi was telling him and Tsotsi in all the time he had known him had been totally without imagination. It must have happened. Why did it happen? What did it mean? Will it happen again, why do things happen? He no longer heard the other's voice, his mind lost in the labyrinth of questions; until suddenly, like the image that rises cool and clear out of the concentric ripples widening away where the pebble has fallen in the water, rising cooler and clearer than ever before, came the thought and phrase again, so he said it aloud: 'The fields of my youth.'

Tsotsi stopped and considered what Boston had said. What did it mean? What was he trying to say? What relevance was there between that sentence and the baby? He broke out into a sweat. I know so little, he thought. I know so little I know nothing.

'And then Boston man, there was the beggar.'

The man on the bed didn't move.

'Boston man.' He waited. 'Hey Boston. The beggar.' Boston looked at him. 'Help me there man. I had him. Really I had him right, but I let him go.'

Boston continued to watch him, so he told that story as well.

Boston concentrated hard, and listened. He heard that story right through to the end. In its way it was as surprising as the other. Why was it strange to find mercy? What a tremendous thought mercy is! The word itself is like the sigh of the wind. Where had he heard it like that? Then it came to him; the long, lonely wind that swept through the long grass in the fields of his youth.

But this time he did not say it aloud. He looked at Tsotsi. He has clenched his hands together in the attitude of prayer. He has beautiful hands. What is he saying? Yellow bitch? Memory of a mother? Tsotsi a mother. Why not, all men come from women. I did. I never went back. She waited for me in the fields of my youth. Standing there, on her hoe in the midday sun, looking down the road. I never went back. Is she still waiting? What is Tsotsi saying?

'I never knew about it. Not till yesterday. Like a long forgetting, you know.' Tsotsi wiped the sweat away from his forehead. Boston had been staring a long time and said nothing. He went to the door, and let the cool air pass over his body. He had told him everything and it had been hard. Not having to tell. That had come easy, driven as he was by some inner compulsion to know the meaning of the past three days and their strange events, a compulsion that had started with the baby and gained momentum ever since until he no longer had a desire for anything else except to know. He had told his stories and Boston had listened and now he must ask his questions and Boston must answer them.

He turned back into the room, and fetching his chair sat down next to the bed. 'Boston, you've read the books.'

'I've read books.'

'So tell me man. What does it mean?'

'What?'

'What I told you Boston.'

Boston closed his eyes. 'We're sick, Tsotsi. All of us, we're sick.'

'From what?'

'From life.'

Tsotsi dropped his head and Boston felt the other man's anguish and for a moment it was like a stab of pain that cut through his own in which he was wrapped like a baby in its swaddling clothes.

He stretched out an arm and touched Tsotsi, and waited for him to look at him, and then into those eyes, desperate eyes, he said: 'I don't know, Tsotsi. I know nothing. I am blind, and deaf and almost dumb. My words are just noises, and I make them in my throat like an animal.' Then he gripped Tsotsi's arm very tightly because he was suddenly seeing something clearly and it might help to say it: 'You are different.'

Tsotsi bent forward.

'You are changing, Tsotsi,' and then later, 'You mustn't be frightened. It happens, man.'

Tsotsi bent still closer, leaning forward with his elbows on his knees, until their heads were only inches apart, and in that way he had only to whisper as if frightened that the very walls might hear, wanting his questions to pass as a final secret between Boston and himself.

'Why Boston? What did do it?'

A sudden elation lit up Boston's face; he tried to smile, but his lips wouldn't move, and his nose started throbbing, but despite the pain he whispered back at Tsotsi: 'You are asking me about God.'

'God.'

'You are asking me about God, Tsotsi. About God, about God.'

Tsotsi sat back, keeping his silence then, and in the immediate moments after Boston had spoken, through the last hour of darkness, even when the candle spluttered and went out because it had burnt down to the wood, still silent when later Boston, who had gone his own way with his memories, remembering something clear as the note of a church bell, murmured the first line of a hymn, 'Gentle Jesus, meek and mild', silent through the last hour together when the grey light in the room found them in the same attitudes, Boston on his bed, Tsotsi in his chair, silent finally when Boston had sat up in his bed and, looking through the window at the paling sky above him, said, 'The green fields of my youth,' giving a deep emphasis to green, staying like that, leaning forwards, his arms stretched out before him, and then making his move to the door.

Tsotsi followed him and once tried to stop him. Boston shook off the hand.

'I must get going Tsotsi. I tell you it was green, green man, the grass in the fields of my youth. I must, man.'

Tsotsi looked at his nakedness, and gave him trousers. He offered him sourmilk and bread, but Boston refused. The last he saw of Boston was the figure of a man, stumbling, half running down the street. Ahead of him the sun had cleared the cooling towers of the gasworks. It was a new day.

=12=

Isaiah was having trouble with the rows again. The difficulty lay in trying to keep them straight. The first one had been easy enough, but then it always was. You just followed the fence, and since that was straight, the row ended up straight. It was the second row that did it. Miss Marriot had shown him. 'Just so much, Isaiah. Put your hand down. Yes. That is how far apart they must be.' He didn't need to look back now to know that he had gone crooked. The little seedling he'd just put in was no less than three hands away from the corresponding one in the first row. Isaiah stole a quick look at the office window. He caught a blur of grey hair, so he pretended to be busy. But she must have seen him.

'Everything all right, Isaiah?'

Could he pretend not to have heard?

'Isaiah!' Old man, white hair, stiff legs, can't hear.

He planted away industriously, taking care to measure the spot for every seedling. If she's watching, he thought, she'll see me doing it right. He made a great show of measuring with his hand. He even went back on his tracks to measure those he had just planted so as to convince the eyes at the window.

Isaiah almost thought he had succeeded when he heard the door slam and her light footsteps coming towards him along the gravel path. He immediately thought of the strange, black, block-heeled, laced shoes that she wore and at which he always stared when she spoke to him. Isaiah sighed inwardly and prepared himself. He'd played it all wrong. He should have answered when she first called. Had he done that she might have been content with a few words from the window. Instead of which ...

'Isaiah, I was calling ...'

He waited.

'Isaiah!'

Great pain, long-suffering pain. She could sound it in a way that he had never heard from anyone else.

'Isaiah! What – have – you – done?'

If you hadn't got used to the white, powdery face and thin lips, and heard only those words, you would have thought tears were coming. Isaiah knew better. He got stiffly to his knees and took a quick look at the face before dropping his eyes. The same, complaining little smile was there that he had seen the very first day he saw her. Now he took off his cap, scratched his head and looked back along the row. The last six or seven, which he had planted with such a great show of measuring the right space, were correct; but after that there was a sudden bulge that tapered away to the start of the bed.

'Isaiah!' The smile was no effort on her part. It was there permanently. She looked at the elderly man with round eyes. 'Yes, look what you've done. Now tell me, aren't you a naughty boy?'

Isaiah smiled and looked up at the sky. She amused him sometimes.

'Yes,' she said. 'A naughty boy. Now I did show you, didn't I?'

'Yes, Miss Marry.' His inability to pronounce the last syllable of her name had a strange, disturbing effect on Miss Marriot.

'One hand apart.'

'Yes, Miss Marry.'

'Marry-yet. Everyone else can say it, Isaiah. Now, about this.' Isobel Marriot turned away and he followed her down to the bulge. 'Good gracious me. Just look at that, will you? What were you thinking of when you did that? There's enough space there for a chrysanthemum. Isn't there?'

'Yes ...' – she had her eyes on him all the time – 'Madam.'

'You'll have to take them out, Isaiah.'

'Yes Madam.'

'All of them.'

'Yes.'

'Every one.'

'Yes.'

She waited. He waited. She played with a necklace of amber stones around her neck, and when she'd finished sighing over the crooked row of seedlings, she looked up and over the fence at a donkey cart passing in the street. Isaiah decided again that the white, powdery smell of Miss Marry was repellent.

'Every one out, measured properly, and then planted again.'

And her shoes; where did she get those shoes?

'And remember, one hand.'

Her legs were like broomsticks.

'Well, get to work you naughty boy.'

Isaiah got down on his knees and the laborious job of replanting every one of the seedlings was begun. He worked determinedly, hoping she would be satisfied and go away. More than anything else, he disliked having her watch him work. He could do nothing or something simple like weeding a garden or planting for hours on end and not notice the time, because of his memories. But with Miss Marriot standing over him, the seconds crawled past like tortoises, while he waited for the next sigh of regret or the sound of her voice in another gentle complaint. Despite his show of diligence and industry, that is what happened now.

'Gently with the roots, Isaiah. They're delicate little things, and we don't want them to die, do we?' Pause. 'Do we, Isaiah?'

'No Madam.'

'Well, if you do it that way, they will. Oh dear!'

Isaiah wiped the sweat off his forehead. What had he done?

'There you go and do it again? Here, let me show you.'

This was the worst of all the unpleasant things that could happen when she was around. She was going to show him. She was going to get down on her knees beside him on the earth, and touch his hand with her thin, cold fingers, and show him. It never worked, because he either closed his eyes or turned his head. Once when she had done that Isaiah had accidentally looked down her dress and seen the flat, white breasts with nipples the size of a tickey. Another time she had farted. Since then he'd never liked being in any intimate proximity with her.

'Are you watching, Isaiah?'

'Yes Madam.'

'Now were you doing it this way?'

'No Madam.'

To an incredible extent a peaceful existence was dependent upon knowing just when to say no or yes to the white man.

'Then why aren't you ...' – and also of knowing when to say nothing at all. 'You know something, Isaiah?' God. She was now busy with her third.

'I sometimes think you don't want them to live.' She said this solemnly, expecting a violent protest. In the silence that followed she crawled on to the fourth seedling. 'Look at this little fellow. Do you think he could live with all his roots sticking out like that?'

'No Madam.'

'Then why do you do it? Sometimes I think you're just a naughty boy.' Using the fence as a support Miss Marriot at last got to her feet. 'There. I've done all your work for you.' Her critical desires were satisfied, but she stayed on for a few minutes longer, looking vacantly over his head into the street where the donkey cart was trotting back the way it had come. She made a few more remarks about chrysanthemums and gladioli and then with a final reminder that he was planting on holy ground, because it was church ground, she left Isaiah.

He had been so exhausted by her presence that he took no more chances. For an hour he worked without a break. At the end of that time the crooked row had been straightened out and then he went back to where he had left off. A few minutes passed and then he was out of sight of her window and could settle down to an uninterrupted reverie on that most provocative of thoughts, the white man.

What better example was there of the immense range of experience covered by that one phrase, the white man, than the contrast between his immediate boss, Miss Marriot, and the big boss, the holy Father Ransome. Heaven and earth, it was, if not hell. They had both taught him, or tried to teach him, to do something; Miss Marriot, endlessly, painfully, regretfully, to weed the church garden and plant seedlings in a straight row, Father Ransome to ring the bell.

It had happened soon after Isaiah got the job as caretaker boy to the church. He was weeding the garden and Father Ransome, seeing him, had come up to him.

'What's your name?'

'Isaiah.'

'You're a Christian, then?'

'Yes boss.'

'Father Ransome, Isaiah.'

'Father Ramsy.'

'That's right.'

'How would you like to ring the bell, Isaiah?'

'Me?'

'Yes. Would you?'

'Me?'

'Right. There's a service tonight. Be at the door ten minutes before seven o'clock and I'll show you.'

That night, ten minutes before seven: 'Pull this rope, Isaiah. Go on.' Isaiah gave it a tug; nothing happened. 'Harder.' He tried again and the bell pealed out one note. 'Do you believe in God, Isaiah?'

'Yes father.'

'Deeply. I mean, do you believe in God a lot?'

'Yes father.'

'Well Isaiah, the ringing of this bell is to call all the other people to believe in God. Remember, some are lazy and don't want to hear. Now try.'

Ding-dong-ong-ong-ong. Ding-dong-ong-ong.

That was all there was to teaching and learning how to ring the church bell.

But Miss Marriot and her weeds. Well, he'd had her this morning again. This way, that way, too much, too little, Naughty Boy, why don't you listen, when will you learn ... and all the time standing on two legs as thin as broomsticks in those strange black shoes.

Isaiah first noticed the man at tea-time: Miss Marriot had called his name three times in a shrill, surprisingly loud voice, so he took his tin around to the office and she filled it with tea for him. There was one tree on the holy church grounds – a crooked bluegum near the big gate for motorcars – and in its shade Isaiah always drank his tea.

He noticed the man because he looked tired. The largest part of Isaiah's long life had been spent in hard work and he knew from personal experience the attitudes and angles of really deep exhaustion, when the body can no longer even carry its own weight. He saw it immediately in the way the young man was sitting on the pavement, and half leaning against the lamp-post, and it reminded him straight away of the terrible time he'd once spent as a labourer on a potato farm. He saw again the terrible, unspeaking postures of his fellow workers, slumped around the walls of the hut where they were herded at night after twelve hours in the fields. From the memory Isaiah might have wandered off into another reverie and forgotten the man opposite him, were it not for the inconsistency of *that* man's being tired. He was the tsotsi-type, the no-good loafers of the street corners and shebeens, the ones you avoided at night, the scum who killed for pennies or tickeys or no reason at all and who never did a day's work in their wicked lives. Yet this one was tired. Isaiah didn't even have to put it as a question. It was there before his eyes. A man tired in a way that he had thought beyond even the hardest worker in the city.

Isaiah knew the warnings. Ignore him. Look the other way. Go about your business as if you have never seen him. But now in his old age life had more than ever before become meaningful in terms of what he could recognize or remember, what he knew or what he had been through himself. So sitting under his tree he swallowed a mouthful of tea and then sighed and said aloud: 'Too much for one man. Shall I throw it away?'

He looked at Tsotsi. 'Somebody else might like some warm tea. What about you?'

The young man sat up and looked at Isaiah, who offered him the tin.

For a moment it looked as if he was going to refuse the tea. Then he got to his feet and came and sat down beside Isaiah. He took the tin with a murmur of thanks and drank. From time to time he looked up and examined the church, seemed to think for a few seconds and then drink again.

'The Church of Christ the Dreamer,' Isaiah proffered.

The young man looked at Isaiah carefully. He seemed to hesitate about saying something in reply, but finally got it out:

'God.'

'That's right.'

'There. Inside.'

'Inside.'

The stranger gave Isaiah his tin back. There was still some tea left. Isaiah hesitated in taking it, but then decided against urging him to finish it all.

'I ring the bell. On Sundays and before evening songs. I ring the bell.' Isaiah pointed at the square belfry. 'You've heard it, haven't you? It's me.'

'Why do you ring it?'

Isaiah closed his eyes with pleasure. 'To call all the other people to believe in God. Some are lazy, you know, and don't want to hear.' When he opened his eyes, he was surprised to see the expression in the other man's face. He was visibly fighting against exhaustion, blinking very quickly and hanging on to Isaiah's lips as if what they had to say was of profound importance to him.

He was about to ask something when Miss Marriot's shrill 'Isaiah' cut into their silence, and Isaiah groaned and looked back at the small white woman.

She came up to the two men.

'Have you got all the marigolds in, Isaiah?'

'No Miss Marry.'

'Oh.' Isaiah got to his feet and threw out the dregs of the tea in his tin. 'Is this your friend, Isaiah?' She didn't wait for a reply. 'You know we don't allow strangers in the grounds.'

She turned to Tsotsi. 'What's your name?'

He got up and walked out of the gate without even acknowledging her presence.

'Who is that man, Isaiah?'

'I don't know, Madam.'

'Well, please tell him ... that this is not a park but a church grounds ... and that he's welcome to pray ... in fact, we want him to pray. Come to me when you've got in all the marigolds.' She couldn't think of anything more to say and went back to her office.

Isaiah went back to work and a few seconds later the young man came up to the fence. 'Have you been inside?' he asked Isaiah.

'What do you mean man? I ring the bell. I told you. On Sundays and before the evening songs.'

'Inside.'

'Just there. By that door. The rope is hanging there.'

'What's inside?'

'The organ. The music, you know. All the seats, and the candles, and Jesus Cries on a cross.'

'Jesus.'

'Inside there.'

'Inside there on the cross.'

The young man sat down on the pavement and they continued their conversation through the fence.

'What's he do?'

'What's he do? Man he's dead.'

'Dead.'

'They killed. They put him up on the cross and he died.'

'What did he do?'

'His father sent him.'

'Who's that?'

'God.'

'Yes. Tell me about God.'

'Why are you asking these things? Why do you look so tired?'

The young man took his time in replying. 'He's got something to do with me. Tell me about God, old man.'

Isaiah wiped the sweat off his forehead. He was enjoying himself.

'God made the world. He made everything. You, me, this street, everything.'

'Go on.'

'Let me see; once it started raining too much, and the water rose high and he feared for everything, so he saved it by putting everything in seven days and seven nights into a big boat which was built under the care of a man called Moses who we call the good shepherd who sailed that boat into a promised land. Later Maria and Joseph gave birth to Jesus.'

'Is that all?'

'That's as far as Holy Father Ramsy got. He tells a bit each Sunday.'

Isaiah noticed with despair that he had forgotten about his hand and that the row had gone crooked again. He crawled back on his hands and knees to point where the row went crooked. The young one followed him on the other side of the fence.

'Where is God?'

'Everywhere. Mostly inside there.' Isaiah indicated the church.

'What does he want?'

The old man thought about this for a time. 'For people to be good. You know. To stop stealing, and killing and robbing.'

'Why's he want that?'

'Because it's a sin.'

'What's a sin?'

'Robbing, stealing and killing.'

'What happens if you do that?'

'Kwe! Lord Jesus Cries will punish you. You done those things?'

'What do you mean punish?'

'Give you hell.'

'Kill you.'

'Maybe.'

The young man went away after that and Isaiah thought he was gone for good. But he came back a few minutes later.

'When do they sing again?'

'Tonight. I ring the bell tonight at ten minutes before seven. Why don't you come?'

'Me?'

'Come man and join in the singing.'

'Me!'

'I'm telling you anybody can come. It's the House of God. I ring His bell. Will you come?'

'Yes.'

'Listen tonight, you hear. Listen for me. I will call you to believe in God.'

His body felt unnaturally light. Walking was no longer the weight of his legs coming down on the hard, resistant earth; but a sensation of drifting as if the shimmering noonday heat was running in the streets and carrying him along with it. A warm wind came scuffling around the corners with clouds of dust. He had passed beyond even feeling the sting as the grains of sand whipped into his flesh. He only closed his eyes, but not tightly, just dropped the lids, and then the wind passed right through him, blowing away his thoughts before he had time to recognize them. The illusion of moving without touching the ground was even greater when he opened his eyes again; the buoyancy was spreading beyond himself. There was no longer any weight to the baby he was carrying, wrapped up in his coat. Other people crossed his range of vision in a seemingly effortless motion. Looking up, he thought he saw rooftops lifting off the walls and drifting away into the white sky. Another wind swept through him and he closed his eyes.

Miriam Ngidi was on her knees behind a large zinc washtub when she saw him coming down the street. For the few seconds that it took him to reach the gate, she stopped her washing and waited, resting on her outstretched arms which were up to their elbows in the bluish grey water. When Tsotsi walked into the yard she got to her feet and flicked the soapsuds off her arms. She knew what he carried wrapped up in his coat. 'The baby?'

Tsotsi nodded.

Miriam turned away and he followed her into the room where she took the baby out of his coat and put it down on the bed.

'What's wrong?'

'He wasn't hungry.'

'That's not so!' Miriam protested. 'He's more hungry than my Simon. Babies need milk. Did you give him the milk in the bottle?'

Tsotsi had sat down on a chair. 'Yes.' To his own ears his voice seemed to come floating from a long distance away. 'I gave it to him. He threw it up.' He remembered now and looked at his hands. The clotted milk had dried on his hands in white, flaky streaks. He started rubbing it off. The bedsprings creaked behind him as Miriam sat down beside the baby and began to work. Tsotsi turned and watched her. She knew exactly what to do. It was an all-enveloping satisfaction

· 146 ·

to watch her and the firm, assured movements of her hands.

'Have you got any money?'

Money? Boston, sourmilk and bread. 'No. No money.' He heard the chink of coins in a cup and then her bare feet on the floor as she crossed the room. She was gone for about ten minutes. In that time he looked out of the door at the tub of washing with which she had been busy when he arrived. Beside it was a bucket piled high with twisted rolls of the washing she had already rinsed out. The thought of the cool water in the tub, of wetness against the skin, of something gurgling thirstily down the throat tormented him. Tsotsi found a bucket of water in one corner and a mug beside it. He took a deep drink and then went back to his chair.

Miriam returned with a small bottle. At the table where he sat she measured out a few tablespoonfuls of a dark brown liquid in a cup and then stirred in a little water.

'Medicine?'

'For the stomach.' She fed it to the baby in spoonfuls and after that she gave him a feeding bottle full of milk. 'A man doesn't know,' she said. 'About babies there are things a man doesn't know and can't do.' She paused and looked at Tsotsi carefully. 'What is the matter with you?'

'Nothing.'

'Your eyes ...' He waited for her to finish. 'You look tired.'

He shrugged his shoulders.

She dropped her eyes to her hand for a few seconds, then looked up suddenly. 'Have you eaten? I've got some bread here.'

Miriam didn't wait for an answer. Tsotsi took one of the slices smeared with dripping that she put down before him. After that she went and checked up on the baby. He was still drinking. Miriam sat down beside him on the bed and spoke from there.

'When I first saw this little one, this baby David, and I knew what you wanted from me it was worse than if ...'

Tsotsi was listening to her carefully.

'You know,' she asked.

'I know.'

'It was worse than that. Because I got a man. My Simon's got a father. Only, we don't know where he is – my husband – Simon's father. His name was Simon too, and I been looking for him, for a long time. I been looking, but he's just gone. So instead I find this little baby David one day in your room and when I knew what you wanted ... you know what I thought. But what I want to say is this.

· 147 ·

I was wrong. Milk goes sour, you know. Mother's milk goes sour too. Mine was. In me. In my tits. It was going sour with all the keeping of it, because Simon's taking food now, and I got more than I need. You understand what I'm saying.'

Tsotsi nodded.

'So it was wrong to keep it you see, I mean to want to keep it. Because you can't, can you? You can't keep everything without it going sour. That is how it was with me – and that is what this little David taught me. You see ...'

Miriam closed her eyes and sighed and with her hands clasped in her lap rocked silently on the bed for a few moments before continuing. 'You see ... I don't think Simon's coming back. I think my man is dead.' It was out. 'I think he's dead and buried somewhere.'

Out at last. In a sudden surge of almost masochistic courage she forced herself to say it again. 'I'm thinking these days that it's almost sure he's dead. Simon is dead.'

She opened her eyes and found Tsotsi staring at her. 'Dead. Simon is dead.'

Miriam looked down at the baby beside her. He'd finished his milk, so she picked him up and rocked him on her knees and rubbed his back and after he'd broken a few winds she put him down again and he went to sleep. None of this interrupted her chain of thought. She picked up where she had left off.

'So Simon is dead, but I got my baby and there's little David too. It's hard times but I'm doing washing and my brother gives me something each week and I manage.' Miriam stood at the door, looking out into the yard. 'I mean, we got to live. Little David – he's got to live. Anyway, Simon must and me too. Even you. We just got to live. Isn't that so? That's what it is. That's all it is. Tomorrow comes and you got to live.'

Tomorrow comes, Tsotsi thought, and a little boy has got no father and his mother never came back and anyway he didn't remember, but tomorrow taught him that he had to live. She was right.

Miriam hesitated for a few seconds at the doorway. When she spoke again her voice was calm and the emotion that had been trembling under it had passed.

'You are tired. You can rest here if you want to.'

She went into the yard and down on her knees, and the heavy silence was broken by the splash and slap of her labours at the tub. There wasn't much left to be washed, and when the last had been rinsed out she dragged the bath to one side and began hanging up the washing to dry. Miriam shook out each piece of washing before draping it over a line.

The whiteness leapt and dazzled in the sunlight. The wind trailed endlessly through them and they billowed out and fluttered as brave as flags. Soon there wasn't a square inch of the yard that wasn't covered with the restless whiteness. Miriam moved through it all, bent low at the waist like someone struggling through a snowstorm. One shirt in particular held his eyes; the sleeves swinging uselessly at the sides, the collar fallen forward as if the man who had worn it had been decapitated.

Soon Miriam was clearing the line and then turned and came towards the room with her arm piled high with the dry washing.

Tsotsi went to the bed and looked down. His baby was awake, but lying quite still. He felt Miriam come up behind him.

'You want to take him. Please don't.'

'Why not?'

'Not ever. Please.'

'Is there water?' She gave him a mug.

'When will you be back?'

'Some time.'

'Where are you going?'

Ding-dong-ong-ong. Ding-dong-ong-ong.

Tsotsi did not yet trust her sufficiently to leave the baby in her care. By nightfall he had returned the baby to the ruins.

He woke up late the next morning. He had slept long. The sun had cleared the rooftops and was already hot.

It was a new day and what he had thought out last night was still there, inside him. Only one thing was important to him now. 'Come back,' the woman had said. 'Come back, Tsotsi.'

I must correct her, he thought. 'My name is David Madondo.'

He said it aloud in the almost empty street, and laughed. The man delivering milk heard him, and looking up said, 'Peace my brother.'

'Peace be with you,' David Madondo replied and carried on his way.

He heard the bulldozers and saw the dust a long way away. It was a strange noise, and he had been hearing it for a long time. When he turned the corner and saw them, he stopped and stared.

The slum clearance had entered a second and decisive stage. The white township had grown impatient. The ruins, they said, were being built up again and as many were still coming in as they carried off in lorries to the new locations or in vans to the jails. So they had sent in the bulldozers to raze the buildings completely to the ground.

He started running from the bottom of the street, and half way up he started shouting: 'No! Stop! Stop it!'

People stopped and watched him pass, and because of the look in his eyes turned and followed him. A few cried 'Stop' with him, but not knowing why.

He jumped through the ruins, leaving the others behind because they weren't going in there, and because of the noise and the dust. Those who were inside, waiting with sledge-hammers behind the bulldozer, they did not hear or see him. They were watching the wall, and it was with something like sadness because they all remembered MaRhabatse.

He got there with seconds to spare. He had enough time to dive for the corner where the baby was hidden, before the first crack snaked along the wall and the topmost bricks came falling down, time enough even then to look, and then finally to remember. Then it was too late for anything; and the wall came down on top of him, flattening him into the dust.

They unearthed him minutes later. All agreed that his smile was beautiful, and strange for a tsotsi, and that when he lay there on his back in the sun, before someone had fetched a blanket, they agreed that it was hard to believe what the back of his head looked like when you saw the smile.

A CHOICE OF PENGUIN FICTION

Monsignor Quixote   Graham Greene

Now filmed for television, Graham Greene's novel, like Cervantes' seventeenth-century classic, is a brilliant fable for its times. 'A deliciously funny novel' – *The Times*

The Dearest and the Best   Leslie Thomas

In the spring of 1940 the spectre of war turned into grim reality – and for all the inhabitants of the historic villages of the New Forest it was the beginning of the most bizarre, funny and tragic episode of their lives. 'Excellent' – *Sunday Times*

Earthly Powers   Anthony Burgess

Anthony Burgess's magnificent masterpiece, an enthralling, epic narrative spanning six decades and spotlighting some of the most vivid events and characters of our times. 'Enormous imagination and vitality . . . a huge book in every way' – Bernard Levin in the *Sunday Times*

The Penitent   Isaac Bashevis Singer

From the Nobel Prize-winning author comes a powerful story of a man who has material wealth but feels spiritually impoverished. 'Singer . . . restates with dignity the spiritual aspirations and the cultural complexities of a lifetime, and it must be said that in doing so he gives the Evil One no quarter and precious little advantage' – Anita Brookner in the *Sunday Times*

Paradise Postponed   John Mortimer

'Hats off to John Mortimer. He's done it again' – *Spectator*. A rumbustious, hilarious new novel from the creator of Rumpole, *Paradise Postponed* is now a major Thames Television series.

Animal Farm   George Orwell

The classic political fable of the twentieth century.

A CHOICE OF PENGUIN FICTION

Maia Richard Adams

The heroic romance of love and war in an ancient empire from one of our greatest storytellers. 'Enormous and powerful' – *Financial Times*

The Warning Bell Lynne Reid Banks

A wonderfully involving, truthful novel about the choices a woman must make in her life – and the price she must pay for ignoring the counsel of her own heart. 'Lynne Reid Banks knows how to get to her reader: this novel grips like Super Glue' – *Observer*

Doctor Slaughter Paul Theroux

Provocative and menacing – a brilliant dissection of lust, ambition and betrayal in 'civilized' London. 'Witty, chilly, exuberant, graphic' – *The Times Literary Supplement*

July's People Nadine Gordimer

Set in South Africa, this novel gives us an unforgettable look at the terrifying, tacit understanding and misunderstandings between blacks and whites. 'This is the best novel that Miss Gordimer has ever written' – Alan Paton in the *Saturday Review*

Wise Virgin A. N. Wilson

Giles Fox's work on the Pottle manuscript, a little-known thirteenth-century tract on virginity, leads him to some innovative research on the subject that takes even his breath away. 'A most elegant and chilling comedy' – *Observer* Books of the Year

Last Resorts Clare Boylan

Harriet loved Joe Fischer for his ordinariness – for his ordinary suits and hats, his ordinary money and his ordinary mind, even for his ordinary wife. 'An unmitigated delight' – *Time Out*

The Collected Stories of Elizabeth Bowen

Seventy-nine stories – love stories, ghost stories, stories of childhood and of London during the Blitz – which all prove that 'the instinctive artist is there at the very heart of her work' – Angus Wilson

Tarr   Wyndham Lewis

A strange picture of a grotesque world where human relationships are just fodder for a master race of artists, Lewis's extraordinary book remains 'a masterpiece of the period' – V. S. Pritchett

Chéri and The Last of Chéri   Colette

Two novels that 'form the classic analysis of a love-affair between a very young man and a middle-aged woman' – Raymond Mortimer

Selected Poems 1923–1967   Jorge Luis Borges

A magnificent bilingual edition of the poetry of one of the greatest writers of today, conjuring up a unique world of invisible roses, uncaught tigers . . .

Beware of Pity   Stefan Zweig

A cavalry officer becomes involved in the suffering of a young girl; when he attempts to avoid the consequences of his behaviour, the results prove fatal . . .

Valmouth and Other Novels   Ronald Firbank

The world of Ronald Firbank – vibrant, colourful and fantastic – is to be found beneath soft deeps of velvet sky dotted with cognac clouds.

Death of a Salesman Arthur Miller

One of the great American plays of the century, this classic study of failure brings to life an unforgettable character: Willy Loman, the shifting and inarticulate hero who is nonetheless a unique individual.

The Echoing Grove Rosamund Lehmann

'No English writer has told of the pains of women in love more truly or more movingly than Rosamund Lehmann' – Marghenita Laski. 'This novel is one of the most absorbing I have read for years' – Simon Raven, *Listener*

Pale Fire Vladimir Nabokov

This book contains the last poem by John Slade, together with a Preface, notes and Index by his posthumous editor. But is the eccentric editor more than just haughty and intolerant – mad, bad, perhaps even dangerous . . .?

The Man Who Was Thursday G. K. Chesterton

This hilarious extravaganza concerns a secret society of revolutionaries sworn to destroy the world. But when Thursday turns out to be not a poet but a Scotland Yard detective, one starts to wonder about the identity of the others . . .

The Rebel Albert Camus

Camus's 'attempt to understand the time I live in' tries to justify innocence in an age of atrocity. 'One of the vital works of our time, compassionate and disillusioned, intelligent but instructed by deeply felt experience' – *Observer*

Letters to Milena Franz Kafka

Perhaps the greatest collection of love letters written in the twentieth century, they are an orgy of bliss and despair, of ecstasy and desperation poured out by Kafka in his brief two-year relationship with Milena Jesenska.

The Age of Reason   Jean-Paul Sartre

The first part of Sartre's classic trilogy, set in the volatile Paris summer of 1938, is itself 'a dynamic, deeply disturbing novel' (Elizabeth Bowen) which tackles some of the major issues of our time.

Three Lives   Gertrude Stein

A turning point in American literature, these portraits of three women – thin, worn Anna, patient, gentle Lena and the complicated, intelligent Melanctha. – represented in 1909 one of the pioneering examples of modernist writing.

Doctor Faustus   Thomas Mann

Perhaps the most convincing description of an artistic genius ever written, this portrait of the composer Leverkuhn is a classic statement of one of Mann's obsessive themes: the discord between genius and sanity.

The New Machiavelli   H. G. Wells

This autobiography of a man who has thrown up a glittering political career and marriage to go into exile with the woman he loves also contains an illuminating Introduction by Melvyn Bragg.

The Collected Poems of Stevie Smith

Amused, amusing and deliciously barbed, this volume includes many poems which dwell on death; as a whole, though, as this first complete edition in paperback makes clear, Smith's poetry affirms an irrepressible love of life.

Rhinoceros / The Chairs / The Lesson   Eugène Ionesco

Three great plays by the man who was one of the founders of what has come to be known as the Theatre of the Absurd.

FOR THE BEST IN PAPERBACKS, LOOK FOR THE 🐧

PENGUIN MODERN CLASSICS

The Second Sex Simone de Beauvoir

This great study of Woman is a landmark in feminist history, drawing together insights from biology, history and sociology as well as literature, psychoanalysis and mythology to produce one of the supreme classics of the twentieth century.

The Bridge of San Luis Rey Thornton Wilder

On 20 July 1714 the finest bridge in all Peru collapsed, killing 5 people. Why? Did it reveal a latent pattern in human life? In this beautiful, vivid and compassionate investigation, Wilder asks some searching questions in telling the story of the survivors.

Parents and Children Ivy Compton-Burnett

This richly entertaining introduction to the world of a unique novelist brings to light the deadly claustrophobia within a late-Victorian upper-middle-class family . . .

Vienna 1900 Arthur Schnitzler

These deceptively languid sketches, four 'games with love and death', lay bare an astonishing and disturbing world of sexual turmoil (which anticipates Freud's discoveries) beneath the smooth surface of manners and convention.

Confessions of Zeno Italo Svevo

Zeno, an innocent in a corrupt world, triumphs in the end through his stoic acceptance of his own failings in this extraordinary, experimental novel which fuses memory, obsession and desire.

The House of Mirth Edith Wharton

Lily Bart – beautiful, intelligent and charming – is trapped like a butterfly in the inverted jam jar of wealthy New York society . . . This tragic comedy of manners was one of Wharton's most shocking and innovative books.

A Confederacy of Dunces   John Kennedy Toole

In this Pulitzer-Prize-winning novel, in the bulky figure of Ignatius J. Reilly, an immortal comic character is born. 'I succumbed, stunned and seduced . . . it is a masterwork of comedy' – *The New York Times*

The Labyrinth of Solitude   Octavio Paz

Nine remarkable essays by Mexico's finest living poet: 'A profound and original book . . . with Lowry's *Under the Volcano* and Eisenstein's *Que Viva Mexico!*, *The Labyrinth of Solitude* completes the trinity of master-works about the spirit of modern Mexico' – *Sunday Times*

Falconer   John Cheever

Ezekiel Farragut, fratricide with a heroin habit, comes to Falconer Correctional Facility. His freedom is enclosed, his view curtailed by iron bars. But he is a man, none the less, and the vice, misery and degradation of prison change a man . . .

The Memory of War and Children in Exile: (Poems 1968–83)   James Fenton

'James Fenton is a poet I find myself again and again wanting to praise' – *Listener*. 'His assemblages bring with them tragedy, comedy, love of the world's variety, and the sadness of its moral blight' – *Observer*

The Bloody Chamber   Angela Carter

In tales that glitter and haunt – strange nuggets from a writer whose wayward pen spills forth stylish, erotic, nightmarish jewels of prose – the old fairy stories live and breathe again, subtly altered, subtly changed.

Cannibalism and the Common Law   A. W. Brian Simpson

In 1884 Tod Dudley and Edwin Stephens were sentenced to death for killing their shipmate in order to eat him. A. W. Brian Simpson unfolds the story of this macabre case in 'a marvellous rangy, atmospheric, complicated book . . . an irresistible blend of sensation and scholarship' – Jonathan Raban in the *Sunday Times*

FOR THE BEST IN PAPERBACKS, LOOK FOR THE 🐧

KING PENGUIN

Bedbugs Clive Sinclair

'Wildly erotic and weirdly plotted, the subconscious erupting violently into everyday life . . . It is not for the squeamish or the lazy. His stories work you hard; tease and torment and shock you' – *Financial Times*

The Awakening of George Darroch Robin Jenkins

An eloquent and powerful story of personal and political upheaval, the one inextricably linked with the other, written by one of Scotland's finest novelists.

In Custody Anita Desai

Deven, a lecturer in a small town in Northern India, is resigned to a life of mediocrity and empty dreams. When asked to interview the greatest poet of Delhi, Deven discovers a new kind of dignity, both for himself and his dreams.

Collected Poems Geoffrey Hill

'Among our finest poets, Geoffrey Hill is at present the most European – in his Latinity, in his dramatization of the Christian condition, in his political intensity . . . The commanding note is unmistakable' – George Steiner in the *Sunday Times*

Parallel Lives Phyllis Rose

In this study of five famous Victorian marriages, including that of John Ruskin and Effie Gray, Phyllis Rose probes our inherited myths and assumptions to make us look again at what we expect from our marriages.

Lamb Bernard MacLaverty

In the Borstal run by Brother Benedict, boys are taught a little of God and a lot of fear. Michael Lamb, one of the brothers, runs away and takes a small boy with him. As the outside world closes in around them, Michael is forced to an uncompromising solution.